This Time Around

Harper Rae James

Dedication

F OR ANYONE WHO HAS lost sight of their self-worth, just remember how badass you truly are, Sis! Fuck the noise—be unapologetically you!

Trigger Warning

DEAR READER,

Before you step into this story, I want you to know that it holds deep emotions, messy love, and characters who are trying to heal in their own imperfect ways. Throughout their journey, you'll find angst and emotional pain tied to both past and present heartbreak, as well as the complicated process of learning to trust and love again.

This book also explores intimacy, including sexual exploration with toys, as the characters discover themselves and each other in new ways.

There is a physical altercation between two characters, moments shaped by grief and loss, and family conflict that makes love feel both fragile and fiercely worth fighting for.

If any of these themes are tender spots for you, please take care of yourself as you read. This story is filled with love, resilience, and healing—but only you know what feels right for your heart. No matter what, you are not alone.

With love,
Harper Rae

Playlist

F OR AN IMMERSIVE READING experience, please enjoy the playlist on Spotify.

https://tr.ee/XEOFMFKAfI

Happy Reading,
Harper Rae

Prologue

"FUCK, YES! RIGHT THERE, don't stop, don't stop, Cash."

I chant his name over and over in my mind as Cash Easton fucks me, the force barreling into me, making contact with the perfect spot deep inside me with each thrust. He just might actually have the largest dick I have ever encountered and holy shit, does he know how to use it. When he pulls out of me, laying slow kisses down my body, an unwelcome emptiness replaces the full sensation I was adjusting to. The hollow void lingers in the air with a palpable absence, as though something vital has been torn away.

"No, what are you doing?" I ask, disappointed as he lowers me to my back.

A slow roll of his tongue over my clit, and I have my answer.

Since the age of 15, some have characterized me as more on the promiscuous side, happily engaging in sexual exploration. I would say I'm comfortable with my sexuality. One time was all it took. The intensity of every sensation being heightened as an orgasm builds within me is electrifying. I decided then that feeling like I needed to justify my desire for orgasms was a waste of time. Besides, the only people with thoughts about it are usually those who aren't getting any anyway.

I love sex. So right now, I am completely content with the fact that I only met Cash a few hours ago. As I gaze down at him through lust coated eyes, seeing him buried between my legs, his mouth glistening with my arousal, I want nothing else but him.

"Bend over so I can watch your fine fucking ass bounce, Blake," he demands as he sits up, placing all his weight on his heels as he leans back. "I want to see every fucking inch of your body." Without question, I pull myself onto all fours on the bed in my hotel room. I prop my arms on the headboard and arch my back, just far enough so I know every inch is on display. I even give it a little wiggle for good measure, and the moan spilling from his lips is pure sex. A devilish grin spreads across my lips.

"I want you back inside me," I pant, peeking over my shoulder.

"I want to play with your ass," Cash whispers in my ear as he runs his hands over the swell of each cheek.

His request makes me pause a moment, surprised by his boldness. "How about you fuck my pussy? It's nice and wet." Again, I wiggle my ass in his direction. I know a lot of guys love ass play, and in the right setting, I'm all for it. But tonight, after a long day at the wedding, with a stranger, no thanks.

He doesn't argue; he doesn't push the issue; instead, he slides down between my legs and goes back to working my pussy with his magical tongue. He lays slow strokes of his tongue across my clit as he licks it from behind, and before he quickens the pace, he slips me onto my back again. Cash is gorgeous, and I'm not sure if it's the alcohol or just the way he is, but he is indecisive as hell in bed, moving positions at rapid fire. I send up a prayer for the former because he's too pretty to be bad in bed.

The thought vanishes as he glides a finger inside me, making an upward turn with his finger, instantly locating my g-spot as if he's memorized its precise location. My toes curl and just as the pressure builds in my core, he takes his other hand and gently pushes down on my stomach right above my pelvic bone. The sensation has me reeling; "Fuck, Cash. Oh, my god!" It sends a wave of warmth surging through my body, electrifying every nerve. It pulses with a thrilling intensity, almost too powerful to contain. The sensation builds, rich, flooding my senses with a rush of euphoria which feels all, consuming, as though time momentarily suspends. As he adds another finger and begins pumping them in and out of my drenched pussy, each touch and each breath amplifies the feeling, sending shivers like a tidal wave from my core outward, leaving a lingering blissful tremor echoing long after my peak.

Holy fuck, well, he just answered my question.

Breathless and panting, I barely have enough strength in me to wrap my legs, which feel like jello, around Cash's waist as he lines himself up, and slides inside of me. His motions start off unhurried, pumping his hips back and forth. Then he changes directions, making small circular motions with his hips, pushing his cock to an overwhelming depth within me. His motions increase as he approaches his release.

"Fuck, Blake," he growls as I feel his cock swell inside me. His whole body shakes as he empties himself. We lay here for a few seconds, both catching our breath.

During the elevator ride up from Knox and Ana's reception, we agreed this was a one-night thing, with no strings attached. Cash lives in San Diego, so we won't see each other once he goes home; no sense in catching feelings for no reason, right?

Right, I remind myself.

So when he got right up, removed his condom, and threw it in the trash can by the tv, I shouldn't have felt a twinge of disappointment, right? And when he picked up his shoes after he threw on his pants and shirt, not even bothering to button it, and walked out of my hotel room with a wave and a half-ass goodbye, it shouldn't have stung. But it did. It fucking stung like hell. It cheapens this night between us, and even though sex is not something I usually fuss over, and I've had my fair share of one-night stands, right now I feel a little used. I genuinely thought we had something here; at least it felt like we did.

I guess in the back of my mind, I believed that all the flirting we did while dancing was creating a connection. We had chemistry, or at least I thought we did. There was a tiny hopeful thought in the dark corner of my mind, maybe after we had sex, a fire would build between us, a connection that would make him realize he wanted to stay a little longer. We would spend the night tangled in the sheets and when the soft glow of the sun started peeking through the curtains, we would decide to get breakfast and our conversation would shift to both of us deciding we wanted to see each other again. We would sip our coffee and discuss how we could make this all work.

How could I be so dumb? So naïve? Guys don't fall for their one-night stand, ever.

After I washed my face and brushed my teeth, I sat down on the edge of the bed as a foreign sensation set in.

Shame: she is a sneaky, ugly bitch!

The Wedding Night

"Don't make a fuss and get crazy over you and me"
-Jennifer Paige

Blake

"**Y**OU LOOK FUCKING STUNNING, Ana. Knox is going to lose his shit when he sees you!" I point out as Ana steps back and beams at me. "Oh! And fuck me, did you see Knox's old teammate Cash? Holy shit, he's so hot!" I add as we place the finishing touches on Ana's hot-as-hell look.

"I'll pass that on to Knox," she chuckles.

The next several minutes fly by as we scurry around the bridal suit, getting Ana ready to walk down the aisle.

About a year ago, she was in a terrible accident and was in the hospital for quite a while. She is quite literally the strongest person I know. As I help her slide the bracelet on her wrist, a gift from Knox, I can't help but admire the scars adorning her arm. They're an intricate road map to all the battles Ana has fought and won, and as I study them, I can't help but feel amazed by my best friend.

Ana and I met at the bar we both worked at and, at first, breaking the shell she retreated into was difficult. Ana doesn't trust easily. Her dad did a number on her family when she was in high school, and Ana is living proof that residual trauma is fucking real. She's spent a lot of time waiting for the people she loves to hurt her, to prove their love was fleeting. She did it with Knox for several years, kept him at arm's length, reacting in big ways to seemingly small things.

Today, watching her find her happy ever-after, is a day I could live on repeat for the rest of my life. I love my best friend with all I have, and seeing her finally happy makes my heart sing.

As I stand at the top of the aisle, the air crackles with intensity, with a profound sense of anticipation and emotion. I tune into every detail as I watch Knox and their son Riker stand together at the altar, their faces alight with admiration and unwavering affection. Every glance they share, every subtle shift in their expressions, speaks volumes. They love Ana more than life itself.

As she makes her way down the aisle, Ana's approach to her boys standing at the altar seems to bring the world to a hush, magnifying the powerful emotions in the air. Knox's eyes are alight with a warmth radiating outward, a blend of admiration and heat is palpable in the crowded room. It's as if he sees Ana not just as she is, but as all she has become and all she means to him-a person who has redefined his world with her strength and grace. Their eyes meet from across the room, noticeably speaking a language all their own-one of an intense love.

I need that!

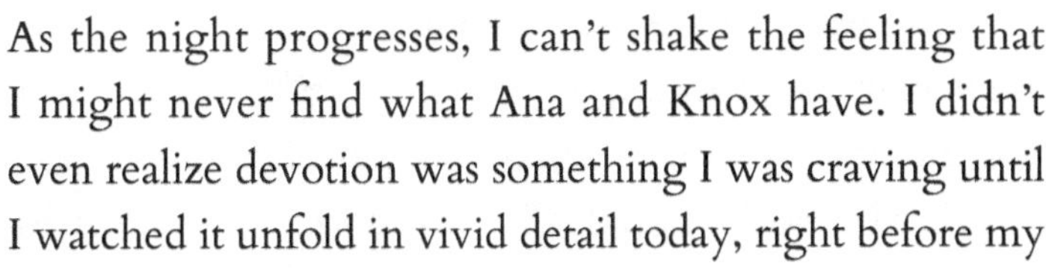

As the night progresses, I can't shake the feeling that I might never find what Ana and Knox have. I didn't even realize devotion was something I was craving until I watched it unfold in vivid detail today, right before my eyes.

"Blake, right?" a sultry voice whispers in my ear from behind, and the heat of his breath against my skin causes goosebumps to erupt in its path. As I turn around, my heart practically leaps out of my chest. Man, Cash is *fine* as hell. I instantly lose all inhibition, falling into my same old comfortable rhythm with men, completely forgetting my internal desire for something more.

"Yep, but if you're looking for more than my name, you'll need to earn it," I answer, lacing my voice with pure seduction.

"Earn it, huh? Well, I'm always up for a challenge. What's the first step?" he asks.

"Why don't you go get us both a drink and we can see where the night takes us?"

After our fourth drink, and one shot with Knox and Ana, every slide of Cash's fingers across the skin on my neck sends butterflies straight past my stomach, direct-ly to my clit. I squeeze my legs together beneath my floor-length dress, attempting to dull the need building inside me.

We have spent the last hour talking, laughing and having a great time.

Now, here we are, slow dancing to "Crush" by Jennifer Paige, and all the other people on the dance floor around us are disappearing like shadows fading at dusk. It's as if the world is gradually melting away, leaving just the two of us in a cocoon of soft, dim light. Each step we take seems to draw the edges of the crowd further into the background until it's just the gentle rhythm of the music and the quiet hum of our own heartbeats, which remain. The bustling energy of the room is now a distant echo, and it feels like we're floating in a serene bubble, where the rest of the world has melted away.

"I don't want this song to end," Cash murmurs, his voice a low, seductive whisper, sending a shiver directly down my spine. As he brushes my hair aside, his fingers graze my neck with a teasing caress. He leans in, his lips hovering close to my skin, so close I can feel the warmth of his breath, but he never quite makes contact. It's a dance of anticipation and desire, his proximity a sultry promise keeping me on edge, savoring every electrifying moment of his near touch. The lingering closeness is both intoxicating and maddening, drawing me farther into the spell of the music and the moment we're sharing.

"No?" I ask, my words stuck in my throat, lost in my need for him to kiss me. I'm completely intoxicated by his existence.

"No, because then, I have to stop touching you."

"Are you looking for an invitation, Cash? Because if you are, I promise, I can make it worth your while."

I don't even wait for him to respond. I take him by the hand and lead him to the elevator, ignoring the glances and whispers from various other guests sitting near the exit as we retreat.

As the elevator doors close, Cash looks at me with lust-coated eyes, "Look, I'm here for a good time, not a long time, ok. I don't want to lead you on. Let's enjoy tonight for what it is."

I blink a few times, flabbergasted by the sudden change in his voice and the slight douchebaggery consuming his demeanor. Yet, I also find myself ignoring that redflag, clouded by the intense need to have his hands on me; Instead, my clit wins the battle, leaving me silently nodding in agreement.

When the elevator doors slide back open, neither of us takes a moment to breathe, our hands pulling at clothes faster than we can move towards the door to my hotel room. I fumble with the key card I retrieved from my bra and slide it over the sensor several times before the green light appears out of the corner of my eye, blocked by Cash's lips on mine. We stumble inside and I forget all about the one thing I really want–a love like the one I witnessed today.

The Morning After

"I wish I was special"
-Radiohead

Blake

Beep. Beep. Beep.

I fumble, trying to reach for my alarm on the nightstand next to the bed. The dim light from the sunrise filters through the thin curtains, casting a soft glow over the room. I squint at the clock. Shit, even with extra time, I'm tired.

After Cash had left, I called down to the front desk and arranged for a late checkout. It was a small indulgence, but the delay was a welcome reprieve granting me an extra hour of sleep, and a little extra time to get ready. It also allowed for an additional buffer to avoid the awkwardness of running into him, the feeling that often comes with the end of a one-night stand. All of it allowed me to sidestep the potential stares and hushed whispers that might follow once the usual checkout time rolled around.

I had a great time last night, but the thought of facing the judgmental glances from other guests as I made my way out was less than appealing. It's a conflict that never quite sits right with me: while I love sex, the aftermath—or the so,called "walk of shame",has always been a different story.

In theory, it's just a part of the experience; in reality, it feels like a lingering shadow threatening the enjoyment of the night, morphing what should be fun and carefree into something more uncomfortable. I hate how people are so damn judgmental.

I turn on the shower wanting, no needing, to wash off the lingering remnants of last night. As the warm water cascades over me, it feels like I'm not only cleansing my body, but my mind as well. The steam and the rhythmic pulse of the showerhead help me reflect on what had happened last night and why I am feeling so damn unsettled.

I replay Cash's words in my head, *"I don't want this song to end."*

He was so into me; why did he leave so fast? Did I come on too strong? Too desperate for love?

I have a hard time placing all of my actions through the alcohol induced fog.

It hits me.

Last night had been more than just sex for me; it triggered something at my very essence, something I hadn't expected. I've always prided myself on keeping things light and uncomplicated, enjoying the thrill of the moment and the orgasms without getting too caught up in emotions. Last night though, something shifted within me. The connection I felt with Cash, the way our conversation flowed so effortlessly, and the genuine chemistry we shared made me realize I was craving more.

I am longing for a meaningful, committed relationship, something I haven't openly admitted to myself before now. Honestly, I'm not even sure if the connection with him was actually there, or if it was simply a figment of my imagination ignited by this newfound need inside me. Maybe it wasn't different with him at all.

Reflecting on my feelings, I realize, the shame didn't come from the sex itself, rather from the contradiction in my mind it created. I set my mind on love, a profound and transformative love, to change my ways and seek something more significant.

"Why do you let your pussy lead?" I scold myself as I rinse the shampoo from my hair.

If I can't keep a focus on what I truly want for mere minutes, how will I ever make it happen? I have to make a genuine change.

I feel better stepping out of the shower having placed an actual reason behind my feelings. As hard of a pill it is to swallow, this self, reflection made me feel a bit more optimistic about the day.

"You've got this B," I reassure myself in the mirror as I throw my hair up in a messy bun, grab my favorite hoodie, leggings, and running shoes, and head out the door of my hotel room.

Running always clears my mind, so I decide to do just that after stopping by the cafe in the lobby for a light breakfast.

"I'm starving, so I'll take my bag to the car after I eat," I whisper to myself on the way downstairs.

I get a table and set my bag in the booth next to me and thumb through my phone for my favorite podcast, "The Best One Yet" by Camron and Samantha. It's a business podcast, and it perfectly blends advice with humor. They keep things entertaining, mixing in, jokes and banter with various entrepreneurial topics and sharing their experiences in starting a new business. The next episode is Marketing, The Art of Creating Content That Sticks. I fucking hate marketing, so I have a lot I need to learn here.

I work at the same bar where Ana and I first met, and let's just say the owner is an actual piece of shit. He struts around like he's God's gift to anyone who walks into the bar, but in reality, he's completely clueless.

If you asked him to distinguish between a mule and a mojito, he'd probably just shrug and offer you a margarita instead. His inflated ego and micromanaging style make every shift feel like hell on earth.

Despite my disdain for him and the bar's atmosphere, the job has its perks, including the generous tips. I've made the most of this situation by using it as a learning opportunity. My dream is to open a bar of my own someday, and I'm determined to do it right. This means immersing myself in every aspect of the industry and gaining as much knowledge as possible, even if that means working under a pompous shitbag.

As a bonus, I'm using my time behind the bar as a hands, on learning experience. I may not enjoy working under the shitbag, but I'm focused on the bigger picture. Every shift, every interaction, and every tip earned is a step toward my dream. The freedom to work for myself and make my dreams pay my fucking bills.

Just as I go to put my AirPods in and hit play, I hear a familiar voice coming from the booth behind me.

"I don't know, man."

Cash, shit!

I sink into the booth, hoping he doesn't see me, just as I hear his voice again.

"Yeah, she's great, but fuck, something just feels off. Maybe I rushed into it. I thought she was the right fit but now I'm wondering if I just got caught up in the moment.

"You seemed into it last night," his friend chuckles, like it's a joke.

"I was," Cash lets out a deep sigh, "I mean, don't get me wrong, she's got a great feel. She looks good, but that only gets you so far. She was just kind of underwhelming, ya know? I don't want to waste my time and money on something that's not worth it. Is she really 'game day' material?"

Game day material? He really is an asshat.

"Yeah, plus you're not really the kind of guy to stick with only one," his friend pipes up.

"True. What if she's not worth the hype?" Cash adds.

My stomach twists in knots. Is this really what he thinks of me?

I can't listen to this shit anymore. I stand up, throw some money down on the table and deliberately flip him off as I walk past his table and head out the door.

Looks like I didn't wait quite long enough to leave my room. Fucking prick!

One Month Later

"Nothing's fine, I'm torn
I'm all out of faith, this is how I feel"
-Natalie Imbruglia

Blake

ONE MONTH HAS PASSED, and the sting of rejection from Cash still hasn't faded. The shame I felt in myself for not taking the time to be true to what I want in my life is still haunting me.

I hear echoes of his words in the restaurant more often than I'd like to admit. *"I mean, don't get me wrong, she's got a great feel. She looks good, but that only gets you so far. She was just kind of underwhelming, ya know?"* I have done a lot of soul, searching over these last few weeks, and I've realized if I want to attract a man who's genuinely worth my time and investment, I need to invest in myself first. This can't happen if I stick with one-night-stands and never truly get to know the other person outside of the bedroom. Maybe Ana was right: *"If you give them all the goods up front, what do they have to look forward to?"* I need to invest in myself too and do things I enjoy. Rediscover me. Spend some time working on me, working on things important to me.

Deciding to carry out my newfound mission, I stop at a bookstore around the corner from the bar on my way to work. If I am going to take a break from men for a while, I will need a few good spicy romance books to help me pass the time.

And a new electric friend. I'll make a pit stop there on the way home from work. I wish there was a place where you could buy both.

As I step into the cozy, dimly lit bookstore, I'm immediately overtaken by a wave of nostalgia. The charm of the place sweeps over me once again. The shelves are a patchwork of mismatched wood and age-worn paint. It makes the space feel lived-in, *loved*. The scent of old paper and books fills the air; a comforting aroma wraps around me like a warm hug, easing a longing I didn't fully realize I had. This is my dream. If I could somehow combine my love for books and mixology, I'd be the happiest woman alive.

Drawn by a burst of vibrant colors nearby, I make my way to a small table in the middle of the aisle. The romance section is sprawled out across several tables, with books displayed like treasures. Their covers are a mix of intricate designs, rich reds, deep blues, and golden accents, and all of them seem to shimmer in the soft light. They picked the perfect books to decorate this display. The artistry of each cover beckons me, promising tales of love and adventure.

I pause, taking it all in, letting my fingers graze the spines of the books as I consider each one. I decide to spend some time here before venturing to explore the more hidden gems on the shelves.

Reading is something I cherish, it's my escape from reality when the world around me gets too heavy. I read a lot when Ana was in the hospital. However, as busy as I am, it is hard for me to find time to really get lost in the pages, so picking a book is something I truly take time in. I don't just read the back cover; I reflect more deeply when considering my choices. The dedication and the prologue, if there is one, are a must. These sections offer insights into the book's soul, revealing hints about its heart and structure.

The prologue, particularly crucial to me, is my first real taste of the book's tone and promise. I love one where it captivates me quickly. I need to be drawn in right from the start, to justify carving out precious time for reading. DNFing a book is not an option for me.

Dedications also hold a special place in my heart. They're like hidden treasures right at the front of the book, personal-intimate, reflecting the author's senti-ment. Spending a moment appreciating these small but meaningful pieces feels like a respectful nod to the writer's journey.

After reading both of those, I quickly scan through the pages to gauge the length of the chapters. I have a particular preference for a balanced cadence. Variety in chapter length provides a satisfying ebb and flow, keeping me engaged without feeling overwhelmed or frustrated.

A sleek black book with gold flecks scattered across the cover catches my eye. Picking it up carefully, I flip through the pages as I make my way over to a small leather chair off to the side of the table. I love the intricate patterns decorating the top of each page and can't help but feel compelled to purchase it purely off sight. I sit down to settle into the dedication when I am startled by a loud voice in my ear and a frantic shift beneath me.

"Shit, umm hello… I'm sitting here," his voice is laced with a hint of surprise and embarrassment, as if he was the one who sat on a stranger. The man seated in the chair I just blindly plopped onto fumbles beneath me, shuffling his way out from under me to stand up quickly. His face flushes slightly as he tries to regain his composure, a mix of awkwardness and confusion apparent in his bright hazel eyes as they shimmer, as if decorated by the sunlight filtering through the autumn leaves here in Vermont. A sight I would recognize anywhere.

"Lucas Jennings, holy shit!" I laugh, throwing myself back into him and wrapping my arms around his neck.

Pulling me back to get a better look at my face, a huge smile takes over his face. "Blake? What are the odds you would literally fall into my lap after all this time? This must be my lucky fucking day!"

Luke and I go way back, though it's been a while since we last saw each other, the Christmas after my 21st birthday to be exact. He's April's older brother, my best friend from high school. April was a welcomed surprise to her parents after they believed they would only ever have Luke. Being twelve years older than us, he absolutely adores his baby sister, and watching him be the best big brother in the world to her made him hot as hell to me, occupying many of my teenage fantasies.

Now, at 38, he's only gotten more attractive with age. The years sure have been kind to him, adding a layer of sophistication and charm that weren't there before. His dark brown hair is now sprinkled with a few flecks of silver, and the scruff once scattered across his face is now a full beard only enhancing his features. Especially those bright hazel eyes. The beard might actually make them shine even more. Luke has always been tall and slender, but I can tell time spent in the gym has filled his 6'2" frame out, but one detail seizing my attention and holding it prisoner are the tattoos covering his right forearm. The way he rolled the sleeves of his sexy button-up amplifies the intricate ink. Shit, he's hot.

Last I heard from April, he was going through a divorce and was looking to transfer to a hospital closer to home once settled. His ex-wife, in my opinion, was never worthy of his love. An opinion formed by the insane jealousy I felt every time I was in a room with the two of them. I couldn't even attend their wedding they invited me to. I hated her. They met during his first year of residency and were married less than a year later.

"What are you doing here?" I try to hide the excitement in my voice. If he's here, that means she's not his wife anymore.

"I was looking through this book before you interrupted me," he answers, wiggling his eyebrows.

"Not here, here. Back from Denver, here," I tease.

"My divorce was finalized a month ago, and I couldn't stand seeing Noel's face every day at work, so I transferred here," he explained, without an ounce of sadness in his voice.

"I'm sorry things didn't work out," I force the words out even though they feel like sandpaper as they leave my mouth, not meaning a single one of them.

"Don't be. I'm sure as hell not. I gave it a solid chance, but sometimes people aren't meant to be."

"Honestly, I'm not sorry either. I always hated that bitch. I was just trying to be nice." Sarcastic laughter escapes me.

"I know and trust me, Blake, pretending you like someone has never been your strong suit," he chuckles.

What does that mean? I wonder as his smell of cedar and mint lingers in the air.

"What are you doing on this side of town?" he asks.

"I work at the bar around the corner," I respond.

"Well… that's good to know. I hear it's the place to go to rinse down the stress following a long shift." The subtle smile spreading across his face heats my core.

Lucas Jennings has never been a real possibility for me anyway-I'm just his little sister's friend, after all, but damn it, of all the times for the most irresistible man I've ever known to come back into my life, it has to be right when I've sworn off men all together. It's like the universe is playing a cruel fucking joke on me, and I'm not a fan.

"Wanna catch up while I finish looking for books?" I ask, sliding the book in my hand under my arm, now more intrigued by his hazel gaze.

"That sounds great." He smiles, and it instantly brings me back to the young girl who had a crush on her best friend's older brother.

"Are you still working in the ER?" I want to know everything about him.

"Of course, it's my favorite. I love the unpredictability of my day. Every moment is a mystery."

"That's a feeling I'm chasing. Loving my job." I give him a shy smile. "I envy you."

"April says you love bartending." He creases his brow.

"I do. It started as a way to make enough to support myself but quickly became a passion. I love the creativity that comes with creating new recipes." I sigh a heavy breath, "Just wish I didn't have to work for a dickweed to do it."

This is not how I want to spend precious time with Lucas Jennings, so I quickly change the subject.

"What book do you have there?"

"Nothing too exciting, it's a memoir written by a trauma surgeon I follow on social media, what are you reading?"

"I'm not sure, someone was in my seat when I sat down to look through it," I tease. "But, I only read romance."

"Interesting." His tone is skeptical.

"Don't be judgy. Romance is the superior genre, period, end of story."

"Why is that?" he inquires.

"Simple, you get to fall in love over and over again, and book boyfriends never fail you." I give him a smug smile.

"I'll have to read one sometime to see if you're right."

"I am right, but why wait?" I ask with a devious grin.

"What?" He laughs.

"Let's pick one out and buddy read it."

"What the hell is buddy reading?" he mocks.

"It's when you read the same book as a buddy, come on Luke, don't be so dense."

I don't wait for him to answer before moving to peruse the shelves, I know he'll do it. I can tell by the look he gives me.

Every time he looks my way, it's as if he cranks up the heat in the room, making it nearly unbearable. This causes me to stay a few steps ahead of him in an attempt to avoid his gaze.

If I don't find a distraction, my toys are going to get a serious workout just to keep my mind off the immediate, fiery attraction he stirs within me.

Luke

I FOLLOW BLAKE THROUGH the aisles of the bookstore, trying to keep my composure. I hadn't expected to run into her today, but since I have, it is impossible not to be captivated by her. Her long red hair tumbles over her shoulders, and the depths of her brown eyes seem to light up with every new book she finds, but my favorite part is the way her bright red lips move when she speaks. It's something small, and has been sweeping me off my feet since she was in college, a sexy little change to her appearance she adopted back then. Every time I see her my mind drifts back, glad it's a change defining her signature look. However, for her, it's more than just her signature look-it's a defining trait setting her apart from every other woman in every room she enters. It isn't just the color.

Though the bold, bright red is eye-catching and un-apologetically vibrant, it is the way she wears it with such confidence; it's sexy as hell. It's as if her lips are a canvas for her personality.

She has several books in her hand at this point, and not one has caught my attention. I've been too distracted to skim any of them over.

I pick up a few of them and pretend to read the back, when all I'm actually doing is taking her in over the cover.

She picks up a novel from a shelf marked "New Releases," and holds it up. "No way, they have it! What do you think of this one?" *'Evermore' by Amber Marlowe* is sprawled across the cover. "It's supposed to be a thrilling mystery with just a touch of romance, plus she's one of my favorite authors."

I take the book from her and examine the cover. The dark design and intriguing blurb on the back catch my interest. "This looks promising. I'm definitely in if you are."

Her face brightens, and she nods enthusiastically. "Great! Let's read this one. How about we meet in a week to talk about it? And then again in two weeks when we've finished?"

Romance is not a genre I read, but I love mysteries, and for her, I would read absolutely anything.

"Sounds perfect," I confirm, trying to mask the excitement stirring inside me at the thought of spending more time with her. It is a simple innocent plan, but it gives me something to look forward to. I need a distraction.

We walk a little more, and I'm surprised when she wanders into the nonfiction section.

"Look at how beautiful this glass of whisky is on the cover of this book. This artwork is freaking amazing. The detail in the ice cubes and the strong amber color. It's amazing," she says, holding out a book for me to see.

"Mixology Magic, huh? I thought you only read romance. Is this for work?" I ask.

"I do. This is for education, not for fun. I've been saving money to open a bar of my own. I listen to a lot of podcasts and read up on different things related to business, mixology, and a bunch of other stuff so I can get it off the ground someday. It's a pipe dream for sure," she shares softly.

"Damn Blake, give yourself a little credit. You are so confident-one of my favorite things about you." I scrunch my brows, "Doubt doesn't look good on you. You're already doing it, you're putting in the work and the time to invest in this plan. That's what it is, a plan. Not a dream. Definitely not a fucking pipe dream. A solid plan, and if you ask me, an amazing one."

She stares at me for a moment and bites her lower lip, sending a wave of heat through me. "Thanks Luke. But how can you be so sure when you barely know anything about it?"

"Because you, Blake, are incredible." I pause, trying to catch my breath. "Incredibly talented, and driven, and you take life by the balls. Everything you do is amazing, and you'll make sure this is too. Now, tell me about your plan. I'm dying to know what's spinning around in that gorgeous mind of yours. I have a feeling it's something I'd love to get lost in." With a gentle stroke of my knuckles across her cheek, the air between us disappears.

Every time she smiles or laughs, I feel a pang of longing, a reminder of the feelings I'd been trying to suppress. Even though she is my little sister's best friend and we are twelve years apart, my attraction to her is undeniable. It is only now, at this moment, I'm finally allowing myself the liberty of submitting to what I already knew-these feelings are more than just a fleeting infatuation, a crush intensified by a loveless marriage. Truth be told, I started falling for her during a visit back for Christmas when she was in college, only cemented in the last time I saw her. Blake McKenzie has occupied so many of my dreams over the last few years and she is pure fucking perfection, always has been.

When we finally say our goodbyes and go our separate ways, I can't shake the thoughts of Blake from my mind. My day at the ER is a blur of patients and procedures, every spare moment filled with thoughts of her.

I remember the moment I first realized I was in love with her during a visit home for Christmas. Noel and I had been struggling for a while by then, and Blake's unexpected presence had brought a brightness to an otherwise gloomy day back home. She walked into my parents' house bundled in a fluffy white jacket and plaid scarf.

"Luke, I'm going to go upstairs and watch tv," Noel said in a flat tone, void of any emotion.

She felt awfully distant, but I hadn't exactly been the most attentive spouse either.

"Sounds good. I'm going to hang out. I'll be up in a bit."

I walked into the living room and there stood Blake, snow dusted her boots and her nose was red from the cold air outside. Her red lips, glossy and full, stole my attention.

I wondered what it would feel like to kiss those lips.

"Hey Luke," she greeted me with a huge smile and an even bigger hug. A hint of vanilla and honey lingered on my shirt for hours.

We spent the entire night laughing and telling stories with April in my parents' living room by the Christmas tree. When dad broke out a game of Left, Right, Center, I realized it had been hours since I'd seen Noel.

"Dad, while you set up, I'm going to check on Noel, see if she wants to come join the fun."

Mom shifted in her seat, and no one made eye contact. I know Noel is not exactly everyone's favorite, but she's my wife, I thought.

I walked upstairs and heard Noels' voice through the cracked door, but her words were muffled. When I walked in she rushed her phone conversation and hung up.

"Who are you talking to?" I asked, though the answer was not particularly intriguing to me.

"Just wishing my sister a Merry Christmas," she said but her tone was flat.

"We are playing games, wanna join?"

"No, I have a headache, so I'm going to try to sleep."

"Ok."

In our relationship, "I have a headache" was usually code for "I want to fight" and I wasn't interested in another fight, so I closed the door and rejoined everyone else down stairs.

The only open chair was next to Blake, and our seamless interactions as we played games were a stark contrast to the forced conversations and touches between Noel and me.

I wished April and my parents would go to bed so I could spend time with Blake-alone.

In hindsight, I'm glad they didn't because I'm not sure I could have kept my hands off of Blake that night, and cheating on Noel was not something I could live with.

I take a sip of my coffee. For some reason, now those feelings feel even more real. Her scent of honey and vanilla linger in my memory long after she is gone, and if I try hard enough right now, I can almost smell it all around me as if it's a lit candle nearby.

A momentary lull in the ER affords me a much needed break. Finally, I have time to just sit in my thoughts about her. I should get a jump on the book she was so excited to read. I find a quiet spot in the break room, pull it out, and start reading. The prologue grabs me immediately with its dark setting and mysterious tone. I find myself so engrossed in my thoughts I almost lose track of time.

As I reach for my phone to text Blake, it buzzes with a text from her. My heart races as I read her message.

> **Blake:** OMG! Just started reading. The prologue is so fucking AMAZING! I want to climb inside this damn book!

A smirk curls my lips as I type back.

> **Me:** I'm a few pages in too. It is pretty damn great. Good pick. I'm already hooked.

> **Blake:** Right! It's like the story has its own gravity, pulling me in. I'm excited to see where it goes.

> **Me:** Same here. It's great to have something to look forward to. Thanks for the idea! See you in a week.

Just as I went to put my phone away, it buzzed with another message from Blake. When I read it, my smirk turns into a full-blown smile.

> **Blake:** I've really missed you. I'm looking forward to our time together—let's make it unforgettable.

> **Me:** I've missed you too, B.

As I set my phone down, I feel a rush of mixed feelings. This book, this connection with Blake, it is all more than I was expecting when I moved back.

My excitement is clouded by a pang in my chest. I'm genuinely curious how April will take this. She used to get annoyed at the idea of Blake flirting with her big brother. Is she going to lose her shit when she hears we're spending time together-alone-or will she be excited we are finally making a connection?

New Beginnings

"I love you more with every breath…"
-Savage Garden

Blake

"**S**O YOU'RE TELLING ME you are going to dinner tonight with April's brother and you're not telling her? This is a fucking date, Blake," Ana declares as we walk down the path behind her house. With all the changes in her life recently, I don't get to see her as much as I used to. I miss her like fucking crazy, so we formed a pact, we'd go on a walk, just the two of us, every Sunday morning.

"It is not a date. We're reading a book together. It's a book club." I smile knowing, for me, it's way more, and Ana knows it.

"Nice try. A book club, give me a break. You've told me SEVERAL times over the years how hot April's brother is. What's his name, again?" she asks.

"Lucas, Luke," I whisper softly.

"Right, *Luke*," she teases. "You have to tell her. If she finds out from someone else, she'll freak out because you hid it from her. She deserves to hear it from you. It will change your friendship. You two just reconnected after being apart for school, and now you see each other regularly. Blake, don't hide it from her, it won't end well."

"How many fucking times can you say you have to tell her in one sentence? I get it. But, pardon me if I have a hard time taking advice from the one person who dismissed mine for almost a year. You did the same thing to Knox when you were pregnant with Riker. Only, that was way worse. You should know how I feel right now. Plus, he's not even into me. We're just hanging out, old friends. Nothing is going to happen. I'll casually mention it to her if he comes up."

"This is a fucking terrible idea, but you do you! Wanna go get coffee?" she changes the subject, knowing this conversation is a lost cause.

"I thought Knox makes sure you have coffee every morning?" I ask.

"He does, and orgasms, but I didn't sleep well, and I could use another cup."

"Are you supposed to drink that much coffee when you're pregnant?" I ask.

"I don't double down every day. Don't judge, we don't judge."

"Not judging," I say, holding my hands up in surrender. "Just wondering."

After my walk with Ana, I went home and looked around online at some open buildings in the area, dreaming of opening a bar in each space. It was a wonderful distraction. There were a few where I could see it coming to life, and I instantly could imagine what it would look like, and feel like, opening up a bar at each location. One of them is an old building with large windows. It has the most amazing charm to it. Weathered brick, exposing the history of the building. There are high ceilings and the bar against the back wall is perfect. Complete with rich mahogany wood and adorned with metal finishings. It's everything I could want in a space, but every time I look at vacancies, I get more and more discouraged. Rent is expensive, and I'm not sure how I will ever save enough to make it happen.

My mind is all over the place as I walk into the restaurant to meet Luke. Maybe I shouldn't have distracted myself looking at listings, but instead thought through what Ana said.

It's been a week, and tonight we are going to talk about the first half of the book we are both reading. I have been trying to convince myself this is nothing since I left Ana's this morning.

I'm glad we've only met twice, because the idea of spending time with Luke now that he is finally on the market, but off it for me, is pure torture.

Only as I walk through the front doors, everything I have been telling myself evaporates instantly when I see him waiting for me. My mind and my body are at war. He is standing there, scrolling through his phone in black pants that appear to be tailored for him, paired with a light blue button-up, and with the sleeves rolled up, it traces every curve of his muscles covered in tattoos.

I want to see those muscles up close and personal.

His dark hair is such a beautiful contrast to the blue, I almost wish this was the only color he owned. As I get closer, the smell of cedar and mint overtakes my senses, overwhelming me, and my mouth goes dry.

"Blake," he says as he waves me over, and just as I approach him, the hostess comes over to lead us to our seats. We chose to meet at a burger bar, and as we walk past the buffet-style counter with cooks lined behind it, my mouth waters, replenishing the moisture I so desperately need.

Luke pulls out my chair and then takes his seat.

"I hope you're hungry," he states matter of factly, "the portions here are huge, and it's all you can eat."

"I'm starving, and burgers are my favorite. I've never been here. What's your favorite?"

"Well, they have three choices. One, you can just order a burger from the grill, or you can go to the buffet and it's all-you-can-eat burgers and sides, all pre-made selections. My ultimate pick is the third choice. It's called

'Your Way'. It resembles a hot pot kitchen. You pick your meat and buns for sliders, and they bring you out this little table grill. You cook it yourself, and then go to the buffet to build your condiment platter and pick your sides," he explains with a smile and it melts me.

"Sounds amazing! How did you find this place? I have lived in this area for years and have never been here." I'm amazed as I look around. The design echoes an old-fashioned diner, with neon lights and fun artifacts scattered about.

"One of my coworkers suggested it one day after work, so a bunch of us came. It's pretty new, I guess, but I loved it so much I've come a few times since."

After we each ate our body weight in sliders and fries, we got milkshakes to-go and took a walk to burn off our food.

"You know, the purpose of this little meet-up was to talk about the book we have been reading, and we haven't even mentioned it once," I sweetly mention.

"This little meet-up?" Luke laughs, "So casual. To be honest, I forgot all about the book. I got distracted by the stunning redhead across from me stuffing her face like it was a burger, eating competition."

"Excuse me. Don't shame me for liking food. You know, cheeseburgers are my favorite. You can't take a girl who loves cheeseburgers to an all-you-can-eat burger joint and expect her to not partake. That's just cruel. It's equivalent to taking someone who loves roller coasters to an amusement park and telling them to just watch. CRUEL Luke!" I emphasize the word cruel with a sassy little smirk.

"Trust me, watching you stuff your mouth was the highlight of my day!"

Shit, Ana was right. There is something brewing between us.

"So, what do you think about the book so far?" he asks in a sultry tone.

"I love it. Amber Marlowe is one of my favorite authors. She builds tension like no other author I've read."

"Yeah, there is a lot of build, up happening. Lots of pent-up energy." He coughs a fake cough in his hand and keeps walking.

Damn it. Ana's going to eat this up.

Luke

T ONIGHT WITH BLAKE TESTED my restraint when it comes to her, and I faltered more than once. As I walk into my room, a vision of her flashes in my mind, and I'm done for

"Fuck," I mutter under my breath as I lazily rub my hand over my raging hard-on. Blake is hot as sin with her red glossy lips, creating pictures which now live rent free in my mind. She was stuffing cheeseburgers in her mouth like a champion eater. Her lips bulged out just enough around her food, making me wonder what they would look like bulging out around my cock, or hanging open in a moan.

I sit in the chair by my window and pick up 'Evermore', but put it back down after a few pages.

It has been way too long since I had a woman in my bed. Noel and I went at least the last year of our marriage without sex, so continuing to read this goddamn book right now, as they start fucking like rabbits, is more than I can take.

Chasing my release, I grab some lotion and head to my bed. I've gotten pretty good at single play, so it won't take long. I glide my hand up and down my length, and just as the pressure builds and intensifies, I picture Blake standing in front of me, her hips swaying as she plays with her nipples. That's all it takes and I'm groaning loudly, spilling my release all over my stomach.

After I clean myself up, I grab my phone and shoot off a text to Blake. Probably not the best choice after unloading my release to visions of her, but what can I say, I'm a masochist.

> **Me:** What the hell, Blake? You said this book had a touch of romance. Fucking like rabbits in explicit detail is not a *touch* of romance.

The bubbles pop up and disappear a few times before she finally responds.

> **Blake:** Yeah… we must be at the same part. I had to stop on the way home from the bookstore to buy a new battery, operated boyfriend. Her books make me feral.

"Christ," I groan loudly. I'm fucking hard again in an instant, picturing Blake with a vibrator sliding across her clit, and now wondering what she sounds like when she comes. This was a bad idea, but no matter how hard I try to stop myself, I fall deeper into her clutches, not a rational thought in my head.

> **Me:** Yeah, well, I just rubbed one out before I texted you. I'm not getting enough action to satiate this need for sex right now, so it's going to be really hard to finish this book.

Just as I hit send, regret instantly takes over. What am I doing? I shouldn't be telling her this. Just as I'm about to apologize, another text comes through.

> **Blake:** Damn, that's hot!

Are we sexting? What is happening?

> **Me:** Sure, but it feels desperate. I can't wait until I see you in person so I can give you a piece of my mind.

> **Blake:** I'm looking forward to it. See you next week.

Fuck, now I'm hard again.

Visions of her go through my mind like pictures in a slideshow, flashing for only a moment before they disappear. Until a memory of her back at my parents' house on Christmas morning settles in, only this one plays out in my mind like a movie.

I went to bed late and woke up early, not something I ever do.

"I'm going to go get some coffee, you want some?" I whispered to Noel as I placed a soft kiss on her temple.

She yawned, "No, I'll go to Starbucks and get one in a little bit. I could use a shot of espresso."

"Just let me know when you're ready and I'll go with you to get one."

I'd go on my own and grab it for her, but trying to decode where she is in her rotating order of lattes is impossible, and we were already on the verge of a fight. I could feel it, no sense in igniting the fire over coffee.

I threw on my t-shirt and headed downstairs. When I walked into the kitchen, Blake was sitting at the counter sipping her coffee, reading a book.

"What you reading?" My voice made her jump. "Sorry, I didn't mean to scare you."

She smiled and my heart quickened.

It was just a look, a soft smile. But it's a look I've branded in my memory. She was such a contrast to the women I left laying in bed upstairs. Blake was warm and loving, rumpled with sleep. The skin on her face was soft and had a light sheen, making the soft pattern of freckles more prominent. They were hard to see, but sometimes makeup made them disappear altogether. I remember wanting to trace them like a roadmap. Her red lashes fluttered when she blinked, and I wondered what it would be like to have them flutter against my chest while she slept.

Ignoring the erection forming, I roll over to go to sleep. I want to savor this vision, I want it to occupy my dreams, so instead of soothing the ache in my pants, I decide to feed the one in my heart as I drift off to sleep.

Last night I finished this goddamn book. I have jacked off more times in the last week than I care to admit. Each time I open the book and a sex scene crosses the pages, I imagine Blake reading it, getting hot and needy. Knowing she has toys and enjoys her personal time is even more enticing.

The thoughts roll around like marbles in my mind, clanking against one another, stirring all kinds of thoughts and emotions. Thoughts and emotions that I can't seem to escape. This book started sensual yet tame. Blake refers to it as a slow burn. I could take it to work with me and read it on my break for the first half of the book, but now, hell no! I'd be hard in seconds and then have to see a patient with a boner. This book became an at-home, only read.

I'm meeting Blake at the burger bar again, and as I'm bracing myself to walk in, my nerves are a shattered mess. I can't wait for this night to be over so we can go our separate ways. Now that we've finished the book, there will be no reason for us to hang out. It's for the best. She's too tempting.

How in the hell do I talk to Blake about the second half of the book when all I have been imagining is her touching herself as she reads it, as I touch myself while I read it?

Fuck.

When I walk in, I see Blake already here at a table, just staring off into space. She looks sad, her shoulders slumped forward, and her posture is curled inward as if she's trying to make herself smaller. She stares at the table, her eyes distant and glazed. There's a heaviness to her expression, a weariness tugging at the corners of her mouth as if she might cry. The light in the room casts soft shadows across her face, emphasizing the expression. Her hands rest limply in her lap, the emptiness of the room echoing the look in her eyes.

"Hey, are you ok?" I ask as I sit down next to her rather than occupying the seat across from her. I curl in close to her, putting my arm over her shoulder and pulling her into my chest so she can rest her head on me.

"Shit day at work," she sighs. "I hate my boss, and he's making me hate the bar. He's such a tool, and without Ana working there, it's been hard, you know?"

She sits for a few minutes just staring into space, and I just let her be, taking in the faint scent of honey and vanilla as she snuggles into the crook of my neck. Then she continues, "Ana hasn't worked with me in a while, so you would think I'd be used to it by now, but I'm not. It sucks when everyone else's life changes around you, and you're just stuck doing the same thing every day."

"Maybe this is a sign. Start putting your plan in motion to open your bar," I suggest.

"I would love to, but I can't just quit. I can't afford rent without a job."

"You could always stay with me-" I cough, we're done hanging out after tonight, I have to remember that. "or April. You know she would never charge you rent if you were trying to start a business."

April, that's a much more rational suggestion.

"I'm not a freeloader, Luke." She gives me a pointed look. "I have worked way too fucking hard to be independent to throw it all away."

Blake never knew her dad, and her mom, she's really something special… She has floated from boyfriend to boyfriend most of Blake's life, and when Blake and April graduated, she bounced. Moving to Vegas with her then,boyfriend.

My understanding is Blake talks to her every once in a while, but the lack of support is why she spent her teen years as an extension of our family. She didn't really have one of her own. She has struggled, and she will not risk what she has built for herself. I should have known better.

I rub her back to comfort her as she places her order and we make our way over to the condiment and fry bar, building our platter.

When we get back to our table I can't help but want to make her feel better.

"Well, I believe in your plan, so if you need help, you know I'm here." I stop there and change the subject to one I have been avoiding. "What did you think of the book?"

"Oh man, I should have eased you into her books. I fucked up, Luke. This is the spiciest book Marlowe has written. But, I loved it. I think the realness the characters show and how vulnerable they are with each other is pure magic."

"She puts a vibrator up his ass, Blake. Vulnerable is an understatement," I whisper a hushed shout at her, and she almost chokes on her water as she laughs.

"When did you become such a vanilla old man?" She has a challenging tone in her voice, like she's daring me to give her a glimpse into things that turn me on.

Leaning in close, I take the bait and whisper, "Trust me, Blake, there is nothing vanilla about my sex life. I just prefer to leave it behind closed doors. I think some things are better left to the imagination, you know?" Her eyes heat and her cheeks blush, and right now I think I'm ok with her picturing whatever she's imagining.

"I-" As soon as the first word leaves her lips, her phone rings. Her brows crease and she answers, clearing her throat.

"Hey, Ap," she greets her, looking at me with a questioning look. She then brings her finger to her mouth, signaling me to be quiet. "Oh nothing, just grabbing dinner with a friend. Can I call you back when I get home?" There is a long pause from Blake as I hear April continue at warp speed on the other end, though I can't make out what she is saying. My sister has more energy than anyone I know. "Shit, I can't wait to hear all about it! I'll call you as soon as I get home, okay? Bye. Love you too."

She hangs up, plops her phone on the table and rests her head in her hands. "What are we doing, Luke?"

"We are getting ready to eat some food," I state the obvious, knowing it's not what she meant.

"No, we're on something resembling a second date, and if it is something I feel like I have to lie to April about, it can't be a good idea," she admits, with her head still buried in her hands.

"Blake, look at me," I gently command, pulling her hands away. "I love spending time with you. You are amazing, but this is not something resembling a date. This is two old friends enjoying a meal and discussing a book. There is nothing else going on here."

Lie.

"You are way too young for me, anyway. You are beautiful, but I don't think of you in that way."

Another lie.

"I just want your friendship. Nothing more."

Another fucking lie.

Pain and embarrassment streams across her face and it cuts through me like a knife, and before I can think better of it, my next words tumble out of my mouth uncontrollably, like a car speeding recklessly down an open road. Only, I'm the one being reckless at this moment.

"Come camping with me next weekend." Fucking masochist. "I'm going with some people from work for one night. I was going to stay two so I could go fishing. Bring a tent, and we'll make some new friends. There is a mix of guys and girls, so it won't be weird. It's also a fairly mixed crowd, so not everyone knows each other."

"No, it's cool. I have some work to do this weekend. Listen, I really enjoyed this time with you. It's been fun getting to know you better, but I have to get going. I have an early meeting tomorrow." She throws down some cash and stands.

"We haven't even eaten yet," I point out.

Shit, say something. You fucked it all up, you idiot.

"Blake, wait," I urge, placing my hand on hers. Her eyes meet mine with an expression I can't place. "Please come with me. I'm the new guy at work, and I'm also kind of the old guy. It would be nice to have someone there, I trust. A real friend. Please."

"Fine," she murmurs after a long pause, "but you're setting up my tent. I hate that shit, and you're buying my burger."

"If I pick up the bill, won't that make this a date?"

"Fuck off Luke." She smiles, and fuck, I'm done for.

That smile, the way it lights up her face, like she knows exactly what it does to me,has me spiraling.

I can't keep pretending I'm in control. Not anymore.

A Step Back

"Don't tell me 'cause it hurts"
-No Doubt

Blake

Y OU WOULD THINK AFTER a week to think it over, I would have come to my senses and told Luke no.

"Blake! What were you thinking?" Ana scolds from the other end of the line.

"I wasn't thinking. That's the problem."

"Do you have feelings for him?" she asks.

"I'm attracted to him."

"Blake, you act like you have feelings for him. What happens when everyone else goes home and you're in the woods with him by yourself?"

"Nothing, Ana. Nothing happens. We go fishing, and come home."

"Have you ever been fishing?" She is clearly judging me now.

"No, but there's a first time for everything."

"You're ridiculous. You've never once talked about fishing, and never would have if he wasn't the one suggesting it. I'll tell you this one more time. This is a BAD idea."

"Well, it's too late to cancel now. I'll call you when I get back," I say quickly and end the phone call.

Ana's warning sets off alarms in my mind, but I ignore them.

Taking a pity invite has never been my thing, but being with him, in any capacity, makes me feel better, happier. So here I am in the passenger seat of his truck, wondering what in the hell I'm thinking.

"90's Alternative?" I ask as No Doubt blares through the speakers. "Are you going to bust out your old CD collection and argue anything after 1999 isn't actual music?"

"I listen to pretty much everything," he informs me in a playful voice. "Don't talk shit when you know it's true. The 90s were iconic in every music genre."

"Ok, old man. What's next? *Back in my day…*" I tease. "You make talking shit too easy. You get all irritated, and your face gets so serious."

"I get irritated because you bust my balls every chance you get. Always have."

"Should I not bust your balls? Would you rather I do something else with them?" I ask, immediately regretting the insinuation I didn't intend.

"Stop it, Blake," he scolds with his eyes glued to the road and the slightest tick of his jaw.

"Sorry, it came out wrong. I won't reference your balls the rest of the weekend. I'll keep my mouth ball free."

"Blake!" he shouts with a laugh and a shake of his head.

I laugh and turn up the music.

Sure as shit, he literally listens to just about everything. He has the most eclectic playlist I have ever heard. The rest of the drive was spent engrossed in the music with little conversion, ignoring the thick tension growing in the truck. You could cut it with a knife, and I'm not sure how to make it less uncomfortable, which is a bad thing. Discomfort makes me socially awkward and I say dumb shit like, *"I'll keep my mouth ball-free."*

I mentally palm my forehead scolding myself for that dumb mistake.

Being with Luke is easy most of the time, but there are situations like this when I end up feeling like his little sister's friend when we're together. The annoying nuisance he has to put up with.

It takes me back to the memories of him being my highschool crush.

"Hop in," he told me, his eyes piercing. It was our senior year, and we spent very little time at school during our lunch break.

April's car was in the shop, and I couldn't afford a car, so she begged Luke to pick us up and take us to the McDonald's up the road.

"Thanks," I yelled over the music.

He just nodded in response, not paying me much attention as he continued to bop his head to the music. I was crammed in his backseat so April could sit upfront.

"I love this song," she smiled at her big brother like being with him was the best thing in the world.

"That's because you're a badass like Gwen Stefani." He ruffled the hair on her head, like big brothers do, and she punched him in the side. It was playful, but she did not find him messing up her hair funny.

"I have to go back to school, Luke." She pulled down the mirror and attempted to fix the giant mess he made.

I sat in the back seat watching their exchange, but every time he moved I could smell his soap, and it was intoxicating. His hair was still wet from his shower, and the way it curled at the ends made him so irresistible.

His phone rang and when he answered it his words felt like a dagger, the reality check I needed.

"Hey, babe… oh, nothing, just taking my sister and her friend to get lunch."

Not even Blake, just his sister's friend.

The feeling of being "his sister's friend" intensifies when we arrive at camp and he introduces me to his buddies from work. "Hey guys, this is my little sister's friend Blake. She works at the bar you guys go to, so I thought it might be nice for you guys to get to know each other." Opposite of us are two guys and the most beautiful woman I have ever laid eyes on.

Her jet black hair is cascading in waves from below a beanie and hits just above her shoulders. She has long black lashes and a natural glow I can imagine is only enhanced by makeup. She catches my eye first because she is staring at Luke the same way I do. I know the look well and every intention behind it. My stomach turns as he leans in and gives her a hug, one lasting a little too long for my comfort.

"Hi," I clear my throat, when my voice comes out unsteady. "Nice to meet you all."

"You're his little sister's friend?" the woman asks. "So you're also quite a few years younger right?"

Luke answers before I can even open my mouth, "Yeah, she's 26."

"Oh man, I remember 26," one guy reminisces, bringing his beer to his mouth. "Those were the days when I was too young and dumb to worry about shit."

They all laugh and my heart sinks slightly as the sound of Luke's laughter reaches my ears.

"We're in our early 30s, Ty. It's not like it's been that long. You're still too dumb to worry about shit most days," the shorter, darker haired guy jokes.

"Sorry, Blake," Luke apologizes as he places his hand on the small of my back. "Ty got carried away before I could finish introducing you. This is Ty, Keith, and Isabelle."

Isabelle.

"Isa," she corrects. "We're not with patients. I like to be a little less formal in my personal life." The words flow off her lips in the most sultry manner, and I find myself captivated by her voice, strong and sensual, just like Selma Hayek. This woman exudes nothing but sex appeal from her voice to each curve you can clearly see beneath her sweats and hoodie.

The three of them walk away after a few moments to start a fire in the center of the tents scattered about. There are about 6 other tents, and I can't help but watch the sway of her hips as she moves. I watch her for a moment as she talks to a tall blond woman by the fire.

"She's gorgeous… and sexy," I point out as he unloads the tents and bags from the bed of his truck.

"Yeah," he confirms, glancing in her direction and then going back to work.

"I think she has a thing for you," I proclaim.

"Yeah? Why do you think that?" he asks as he lifts the cooler out of the truck.

"She looks at you like a teenage girl with her first crush. Trust me, I know that look well."

"Aw, you had a crush on me?" he teases as he bumps my shoulder. "Just kidding, I know you did. April made sure she told me every chance she got."

"Bitch," I joke with a laugh. "Some friend she is."

We joke and laugh the entire time we set up our tents, and when I look up, I realize we are a little farther back than the rest of the group.

"Why are we so far away?" I ask.

"I hate when smoke gets in my tent. I like to be away from the fire. Plus, I'm old. If I go to bed before everyone else, I don't want to hear the noise as much. Do you want me to move yours closer?"

"No. This is great. We can have our own brief escape." I smile.

"Want a drink?" I ask as I bend into the cooler, and when I peek through the space between my elbow and hip to look in his direction, I see his eyes glued to my ass. I'm pretty sure he doesn't see me looking, because he isn't even trying to hide his stare. When he doesn't answer, I look away, feeling the heat between my legs, and ask one more time, "Want a drink?"

"Umm…" He clears his throat, "Sure."

Standing, I hand him a beer and make my way inside my tent. "I'm going to change into something a little warmer," I say.

As I zip the tent closed, a smile erupts across my face.

"I don't see you like that," my ass. I chuckle. The sight of Luke's eyes on me is the hottest thing I have ever experienced.

I change into a pair of black sweats and a matching hoodie, take my hair out of the pony, and run my fingers through it. I hate when cold air brushes my neck. Unable to know how crazy it looks, I decide to grab a baseball hat out of my bag and put it on just in case.

As I emerge from the tent, I hear Luke just a few feet away having a conversation with who I assume is one of his coworkers. I zip my tent and spin around to see Luke's bright hazel eyes looking right at me over the shoulder of the guy he is talking to. The look in his eyes leaves me dripping. The guy's back is to me, and because he is a few inches shorter than Luke, we can make uninterrupted eye contact as he gives me a swift, but not too discrete once over. Noticing it as well, the guy turns around to see who has stolen Luke's attention, and my stomach plummets to the ground.

"Hey Blake, come meet Cash," Luke calls me over.

I stand frozen, not knowing what to do, as the two of them move towards me. The look on Cash's face echoes mine as he shakes his head slightly to clear his confusion and precedes to pretend he doesn't know me.

"Luke mentioned you're friends with his little sister. Nice of him to let you tag along," Cash voices, and I want to punch him in the dick.

"I actually invited her to come with me. She's a great time," Luke confesses, blind to the assumption in Cash's expression.

"I can imagine," the implication is clear in Cash's voice accompanied by his devilish grin before he walks away.

He looks over his shoulder one last time and lies, "Nice to meet you."

I fucking hate that prick.

"How do you know him?" I ask. "He looks familiar."

"Yeah, he plays baseball for the Padre's. You've probably seen him on tv. He's friends with Ty. I guess his team is partnering with a foundation here in town, and he's going to be spending the next few months here off and on to volunteer. I'm guessing Ty wanted him to meet everyone before he starts this week. He seems like a pretty cool guy."

"Yeah, he seems to be. Why didn't he partner with a hospital in San Diego?" I ask in a hushed whisper, raising an eyebrow.

"Cash was looking for an excuse to come back home, and convinced them to expand their partnership. He must pack a big punch to convince them to send him this far."

You have no idea, it'll hit you in the gut out of nowhere.

Cash spends the rest of the night playing it cool, pretending he doesn't know me, so it's easy for me to do the same.

For the next few hours, we all sit around the fire listening to music. I get so lost in conversation with Luke, I almost forget that creep is here, until he stands with a yawn, "It was nice to meet you all, but I have an early morning, so I'm going to head to bed."

"Where the fuck do you have to be so early?" Ty asks.

"My buddy who just got married invited me over for breakfast. I haven't really had the chance to catch up with him since I've been back."

Fuck. I never told Ana what happened, played it off as a casual hook up. I never thought I'd have to see him again.

Does this mean he's going to be a permanent fixture in my fucked up life?

Suddenly, I feel a hand on my knee and exhale loudly. "You ok? You look like you saw a ghost," Luke asks.

"Yeah, fine," I lie. "I'm just thinking about another drink. Want one?" Before Cash has a chance to walk away, I stand and walk towards the cooler.

"Sure," Luke speaks up, with his eyes never leaving me.

"Keep your cool Blake, he's not worth it. Keep your cool and don't cause a scene." These are the words I repeat to myself all the way over to the cooler.

I know I can overreact to rejection, it's a real problem I have. I think it stems from feeling abandoned by my mom, but the drama is in the details, right?

"Blake, can we talk for just a second?" Cash whispers his request in my ear, and I'm sure to everyone around us, it looks like we are just making small talk.

"I have nothing to say to you," I sneer.

"Blake, I don't know these people, I want to make a good impression, please," he pleads.

"A good impression?" I scoff. "Trust me you make a good first impression, it's the ones that follow that you need to work on."

He looks at me like I'm crazy, and it infuriates me.

"What are you talking about? I know you're mad. The way you stormed out of the hotel cafe told me that, but I don't know why."

I let out a sharp scoff, "Yeah, I bet."

Not in the mood for this conversation, I make my way back to my seat, and Cash stands there for a moment before he slowly walks to his tent, calling it a night.

When I return and hand Luke his beer, his fingers brush over mine, sending a shiver through my body. His back was to us, so I know he wouldn't have noticed our hushed conversation.

I can't let Cash get the best of me.

Deciding to let it go for now, I return my undivided attention to Luke. He consumes it anyway, I might as well stop fighting it, for now.

Luke

B LAKE'S ENTIRE DEMEANOR CHANGED when we got here. She's retreated into a shell I have never seen before, as if she is trying to make herself invisible. Quiet, reserved, not talking any shit to me as we sit in uncomfortable silence.

I think she's a little threatened by Isa. She thinks there's something going on between us. As a silent reassurance, I've tried to keep my distance from Isa, staying close to Blake.

I know I can't have Blake, but I still want her to know how amazing I think she is. She kept looking across the fire at the group with tension in her shoulders.

With everyone else in bed, I decide to broach the conversation.

"Blake, I just want you to know I don't have feelings for Isa. I don't want you to feel uncomfortable, like I might take someone back to my tent right next to yours. She's not my type."

"How in the world is she not your type?" She laughs. "Fuck, she's my type, and I'm not even into chicks. She is hot as fuck!" Her words are louder than intended.

"Shhh. You're going to wake everyone up." I laugh, putting my hand over her mouth, and her eyes widen at the touch.

Fuck me. I want to see that look on her face with my hand over her mouth and my dick buried inside her.

"She's great, don't get me wrong, I'm just not attracted to her. I think Noel ruined me ever attempting a relationship with someone from work. It's too complicated." That seems to do the trick. She settles into her chair and takes a long pull of her beer.

"It's so beautiful out here." She smiles. "The view is breathtaking."

"Sure is," I respond, admiring my view of her, not giving a shit about anything around us. It would pale in comparison anyways.

"How is work going? You seem like you're fitting in."

"There were a few hospitals that I was looking at, but this one was one of the top rated for emergency care. It was one of the things that enticed me the most." I left out the fact that while the hospital was close to my family, it wasn't the closest. Being close to her was also a deciding factor. "They get a lot more action than the hospital I worked at in Denver, so it's been nice. I'm learning a lot."

"That's amazing. I bet your shifts go by fast."

"They really do."

"How come I haven't seen you at the bar with everyone after your shifts?" She has a curious look on her face, genuinely curious. "Thought for sure after you mentioned that they all go there, I'd see you."

"You looking for me, B?" I inquire, hoping I get the answer I want.

"No, just curious." She pulls out her phone. "Shit, it's almost 2. We better get some sleep."

"Yeah, that's probably a good idea. You go, I'll wait until you're in your tent to put out the fire, so you can see," I offer.

She rises from her chair, a little unsteady on her feet and saunters to her tent. Each step creates the most delicious sway of her hips, and I can't help but watch.

This girl is going to be my undoing.

I roll over and look at my watch and see it's 8:30. The smell of eggs and bacon wafts through the air, arousing me from my sleepy state, and my stomach instantly growls. I throw on my sweats and hoodie and walk out to see Blake talking to some people she met last night. She fits right in, like she does in any setting, even though she always stands out to me.

Seeing her this morning is quite the contrast to the quiet, reserved version of her I witnessed last night.

She must have just needed time to warm up.

I stand back for a second and take her in. I have seen her in many states over the years, pretty much living in my home when she and April were in high school, but this right here is my favorite version of Blake. She is always beautiful, but her beauty in the morning is effortless, it's similar to the one that caught my eye that one Christmas morning. Sleep still lingering in her eyes, in a dreamlike state. Her hair slightly tousled, skin slightly flush. Fuck, it's perfection. If I could wake up to this sight every day, I'd die a lucky man.

"Morning," she speaks gently as she hands me a coffee. "I was just getting ready to come get you so you could eat."

"Thanks, it smells great. Who cooked?" I ask.

"Ty, he got up early to help Cash get all packed up."

"You been up long?" I ask.

"A little while, the sound of Cash's car driving past my tent woke me and I couldn't go back to sleep."

"You should have woken me."

"I had company," she says smiling at Ty.

"What do you want to do today?"

"A nap sounds freaking amazing. We were up so late, I don't remember the last time I was up that late. I even try to avoid closing shifts at the bar. I need my sleep."

"Hey, once everyone else gets packed up to leave, we're going to head out for a hike, you guys want to join?" Keith's question shifts my attention.

"That sounds like the perfect time for me to nap, you have fun," Blake smiles, urging me to go.

After breakfast, we sat around and visited with everyone while a handful of others packed up to leave. After a few chill hours, Blake went to take a nap in her tent, and Ty, Keith, Isa, and I left for our hike.

We barely got to the trailhead before Keith started in on me.

"I thought you were getting up to fish this morning?" Keith asks. "You know, being an old man and shit."

"That was the plan until I was at the fire until god knows what hour."

"You have a thing for her?" Ty asks.

"Why?" I see something lingering behind his question.

"Dude, she's fucking, She's beautiful," he expresses. "If you're not going for it, you're a dumb fuck, and I will."

"You leave her the fuck alone, Ty. She's a good girl. She's special, ok. She's not just a random hook up."

"Who said anything about a random hook up? If I get the chance to take her home, I'll keep her there." He laughs.

"No shit," Keith adds, "The way she looks at you, if you don't make a move, you're a fool."

"She's a baby," Isa pipes in. "She's too young for any of you fools, especially you Luke," she warns, pushing past me.

By the time we got back to camp, it had been several hours. Blake was now awake, reading in a chair wrapped in a large blanket, with her red hair in a messy bun, and she's biting the edge of her lip in concentration. The sight stops me in my tracks. The sun glistens on each strand of her hair, framing her face, looking like an extension of the fire glowing beside her, the light making it a breathtaking sight.

Fucking stunning.

I have to focus on reminding myself she is off limits.

"Let's get the brats started so we can leave before it's too dark," Isa suggests.

"Brats sound fucking delicious," Blake speaks up over the edge cover of her book. "Let me help," she insists.

I open the package of brats and place them on the small grill. "You can't just raw dog them. They need some flavor, Luke," Blake advises.

"I didn't bring very many seasonings, we're camping," I argue.

"Move over." She pushes me out of the way and grabs a knife off the table. "Can you get me a can of beer and some salt, please?" she directs her question at Ty as she slices a slit across each brat.

When Ty hands her the open can of beer and salt, she uses them both to season the brats, adding a little more beer every so often until they are fully cooked.

"Come get 'em while they're hot," she yells over the music playing in the background.

She reaches for a plate. "I got it, you cooked, I serve," I propose as I load two plates with brats, chips, and all the fixings.

"Shit, these are great," Keith says with a mouth full of food.

"They are exceptional," Isa compliments, but it sounds like she's hesitant to give her this little feat, but then she continues, "Best camping brats I've had."

Hmmm…

"Thanks, guys," Blake responds. Her voice is soothing even when her words are simple.

Once everyone is full, and every last brat is gone, they start packing up their tents and collecting their scattered belongings.

"It's starting to get dark, you sure you don't want to stay another night?" I ask Ty.

"No, we have early shifts tomorrow at the hospital. Good thing Blake came along, or your ass would be out here all alone, and no one would hear you scream if a bear attacked," he jokes.

"Fuck off," I chuckle as we say our goodbyes.

I helped them load up the car and stood around talking shit for a few minutes, but now that they're gone, I can focus on Blake. I grab two beers and pull my chair up next to Blake, who is cuddling under a blanket close to the fire. I struggle to keep my eyes to myself, not wanting to reveal the battle raging within me.

"Are you sure you don't want to pack up too and head out?" I ask her as I slide into the chair next to her.

"I loved meeting your friends and putting names to the faces I've seen at the bar, but I really love our time together, just the two of us. So, yes. I am positive I want to stay another night," she reassures me with a smile.

"I love camping." I sigh. Being outdoors is one of my favorite things.

"Hey, do you remember when we tried going on that camping trip right after April and I graduated. Your dad rented a camper and everything, and then we got record breaking monsoon rains and couldn't make it up the dirt road." She laughs.

"Yes, you and April were singing at the top of your lungs, pissing him off while he tried to back us out."

"You were so calm," she adds.

"What do you mean?"

"We were acting the fool trying to mask our fear, and you just sat there calmly helping your dad navigate down the small hill from the back seat. You were comforting."

"I was scared, but someone had to bring sanity to the party, and it wasn't going to be either one of you, or dad for that matter. He was stressed."

"What was your mom doing? I don't remember her at all." She laughs.

"She got out of the car, said she'd meet us at the bottom. She'd rather risk the rain than deal with our shitshow." I laugh

"That's right, fun times." Her words are starting to slow.

"You sound a little tipsy," I note, handing her another drink.

"It's cold out here, so I've got to warm up somehow."

"Were you cold last night?" I ask as I stand. "I have a few extra blankets."

"Luke, sit down." She pats my chair. "You don't have to take care of me. If I get cold, I can warm myself up."

"Always busting my balls. Guess you don't need me."

"I can take care of myself and my own needs. Trust me, I don't need a man, but I love your company." She takes a drink of her beer and places it in the cup holder on her chair.

"What if I want to be the one to take care of your needs?" I ask. "All of them. I brought you out here, to the middle of nowhere. I should be able to take care of you." Fuck, I'm drunk too. Losing all inhibitions, as I scoot in closer. "I'm supposed to protect you. Take care of you, Blake."

"Luke, I'm not your little sister's friend anymore. I'm all grown up, and I can take care of myself," she reminds me.

"Trust me, Blake, I know you're all grownup. I've known for a long fucking time. There is nothing about you resembling my little sister's friend anymore." I brush her hair behind her ear and whisper, "It's really fucking hard though for me to keep reminding myself you are."

Her breath shudders at my touch, and it makes my dick twitch.

"It's kind of late, and we are both drunk. If you want to get up early to fish, we should probably call it a night earlier than we did last night," she advises and then moves from her chair, kisses my forehead, and walks to her tent. I watch the sway of her hips with each step before putting out the fire and heading back to my tent.

I love that sexy sway, and I can't keep my eyes off it.

Settling into my sleeping bag, I close my eyes, wishing I would just get out of my head already. I roll over and the noise of my rustling sleeping bag echoes. Suddenly, I hear a faint buzzing sound. After a few seconds of it driving me fucking crazy, I sit up. It buzzes for a few seconds, and then stops. I'm guessing Blake fell asleep and her texts are going off like fucking crazy or some shit. Damnit, hopefully it's not April, texting her because she found out we came camping. Reaching for my phone, I realize it's dead. When I set it down, I hear the buzz again. Paranoia sets in. I put my clothes back on and walk a few brief steps to Blake's tent to ask her to check her phone and make sure everything is okay. I quickly unzip the zipper to her tent and when the door falls open, I'm frozen in place, my dick instantly hardening in my pants.

Blake is sitting in the middle of her tent, propped up on one elbow, head tilted back, and the other hand holds a vibrator to her clit. The vibration and sucking sound draw my eyes south. It's then I realize it's not just a vibrator. There is a part of the toy peeking out from the lips of her pussy, making short rotating motions as she holds it in place. The softest moan rolls off her lips, barely audible as her eyes shoot to mine. Slight panic crosses her face, but she doesn't stop as her body convulses. She can't stop, even if she wanted to. She's in the middle of an orgasm.

Right here.

In front of me.

And I can't move either. I just watch, like a fucking creep.

Realizing how wrong it is to watch her, I move back and turn to walk away. I need to get the fuck out of here. My heart is racing, blood running through my veins as if heated by the raging sun.

"Luke, shit. I'm sorry," she pleads, running behind me, holding a small blanket up, barely covering her half naked, perfect body.

"No. I thought your phone was buzzing with texts and you fell asleep and didn't hear it. Then I panicked because I thought maybe April was texting you. Pissed we are here. I'm drunk, and then you were, Fuck. Fucking yourself. I'm sorry I shouldn't have come over."

"I shouldn't have been… Fu… Fucking myself," she laughs. "Next to you."

"You can do whatever you want in your own tent. I, shit, I just stared at you like a creep," I admit in regret, turning towards her and brushing my hand through my hair. Her eyes immediately drop to my raging erection, and her mouth drops open.

"You know, it's uh, It's been a long day. We should go to bed, for real," she stutters, walking back towards her tent, her bare ass swaying in the moonlight.

"Blake. Wait," my shout echoes, and she turns around, trying to lift the small blanket to cover her ass. "I'm sorry. I didn't know what I was walking into. If I did–" She cuts me off.

"Luke, you were talking about how hard it is to remind yourself I'm April's friend, something I have been wanting to hear my whole adult life, and you were brushing my hair behind my ear and whispering things. If you didn't know how turned on I was by how abruptly I left, then I can't help you. I know this is crossing a line, but you turn me on so fucking much. You always have. So if you ever find yourself in a tent next to me again, and hear a buzzing sound, I can promise you, it is most definitely NOT my phone," she promises and then turns to make her way back into her tent and I just stand there, dumbfounded with a raging hard on.

A Different Walk of Shame

"I want to wake up where you are…"
-Goo Goo Dolls

Blake

"Coffee-black, and a blueberry muffin top, please," I place my order with the barista at the coffee cart in the hospital lobby. I woke up early, deciding to surprise Luke with a coffee as a peace offering after the shitshow that unraveled in the middle of the woods. He'd tried to play it off like it was no big deal, but it was, in fact, a big fat fucking deal. The ride home was torture. I have never been more humiliated in my entire life. To make matters worse, my fucking word vomit revealed all of the secret feelings I've been harboring for him.

I also didn't really think this through. I'm not really sure how to find him, or if I will even be able to talk to him. He doesn't have an office, and he might be too busy… So… this could be a terrible plan.

My internal debate ends abruptly when I hear Cash's voice just as I turn the corner.

"Fucking. Bitch."

"Excuse me?" I'm taken back by his reaction. I know I was rude to him, but shit. He looks at me as if my presence pains him.

"Blake, what are you doing here?" he groans looking around to ensure we're alone. "This is my first day volunteering. I can't have this conversation with you right now."

"Don't flatter yourself. I didn't come here for you."

"Fine," he huffs, shaking his head.

"If you don't want to have this conversation right now, then leave, Cash."

"Why are you being such a bitch to me?" he questions in a hushed tone.

"You're kidding, right? I don't know how you convince anyone to fall for your bullshit." I storm off not waiting for his response.

The double doors leading to the ER check in feel like a much needed barrier between me and the asshat on the other side.

"Are you here to check in or to visit?" the older blonde behind the counter asks. Her eyes searching the room behind me for the obvious source of my frustration.

"I'm here to see Dr. Jennings," I announce sweetly. "He was not expecting me, so if he's busy, I can leave a note."

"Can I have your name?" she asks.

"Blake McKenzie"

"Thank you, Miss McKenzie, and what is the purpose of your visit?" she asks.

A peace offering because he walked in on me pleasuring myself in the fucking woods.

"I was just catching up with someone nearby and wanted to bring him this," I explain, holding up the coffee and muffin.

"Let me see if he is available." She picks up the phone and I hear a chime come over the speakers.

Turning red, I place my hand on the counter as she pages him over the intercom system.

"No, no, no. It's ok, I can just leave this here. I didn't realize-" She doesn't hear me, as the phone on her desk rings and she answers.

"Hi Dr. Jennings, there is a Miss McKenzie here to see you." There is a long pause, and then she continues, "Ok, I will let her know."

"He is finishing up with a patient, but said he will meet you in the cafeteria in about 15 minutes. He insisted you wait," she informs me with a smile.

For 15 minutes I pace the length of the cafeteria seating area, biting at the skin around my nails, a nervous habit I inherited from my mother. It's an ugly habit so I consciously replace it with little bites of the muffin I got Luke. He won't care, right? When there's no sign of Luke after 20 minutes of pacing back and forth, I decide to send him a text and head home, tail tucked between my legs.

> **Me:** Wanted to bring you a coffee to apologize for the awkward orgasm encounter. You must have gotten busy. Let's catch up soon.

His response immediately comes through.

> **Luke:** Sit the fuck down and stop pacing the room. You're going to scare the other people.

I look and see him at the cashier with two coffees in hand.

> **Me:** Doubt I'm the first one to pace these floors.

As Luke approaches me, his smile spreads even farther across his face, reaching the corner of his eyes, making them sparkle. I wish there was a version of our reality where I could see him smile every damn day. His smile is the most genuine in the world. It lights up his entire face. It's effortless and unguarded, a stark contrast to mine lately. His lips curl, creating soft lines, creating a soft crinkle at the corner of his eyes, adding a layer of sincerity. A smile that makes me feel seen, understood, and heats me from the inside.

"I thought you might want a hot cup," he offers, placing the coffee down next to the already cold cup of coffee.

Before he sits down, he lays a soft kiss on the top of my head.

"I got it for you, as a peace offering. I also got you a muffin, but I ate it." I offer him an apologetic smile. "Please don't get spooked because I touched myself."

He leans in close, his voice barely above a whisper, "Trust me, Blake, spooked is not how I would describe my reaction."

"I'm sorry," I offer the apology, but it's met with his finger on my lips, silencing my words.

"Don't be." He smiles.

The warmth of his touch lingers, but there's something more in his eyes, something unspoken, that makes my heart race.

And as the silence stretches, I realize-this is only the beginning of whatever comes next.

Luke

I'M NOT SURE WHAT happens to me when Blake is in the room, but honestly, I'm tired of fighting it. I am not a crude guy, and talking so candidly about my sexual desires is not something I am accustomed to, but she awakens this side of me. One I'm getting more and more curious to explore.

"You look tired," she comments. "Do you still have a long shift ahead of you?"

"Nope. Just ended, well technically, it ended an hour ago, but I got caught up with a patient. You have perfect timing."

"You probably shouldn't be drinking coffee then," she adds with a half smile.

"It's decaf tea. I have been having a hard time sleeping, so I know better than to add caffeine to the mix."

"Why?" she asks with a laugh. "Too busy picturing the horror show I unleashed on you this weekend?"

"More of a fantasy than a horror show, but I've just been struggling to find my footing here." She doesn't respond right away, instead she studies me. Concern etches her face, prompting her to lean in closer. So close I can smell the hint of vanilla and honey as it radiates off her.

"Luke, I've never seen you like this. Are you sure you're OK?"

There is an undeniable warmth in her gaze, a softness. It looks a lot like affection. She's worried about me.

"I will be. I just need more time to adjust."

"Luke, if you're even half the doctor I believe you are, they're fortunate to have you here."

"It's just been hard. I had a place there, you know? Credibility and people who trusted me. I haven't been the new guy in a long time, and now..." I pause, not knowing what I'm even thinking. She doesn't expect me to continue. She just stands up and scoots in close to me.

Without a word, she places her head on my shoulder, grabs my hand between hers, and lightly glides her fingers over each knuckle. It's a soft yet intimate action. An action likely to be exchanged between two people madly in love, who care deeply for one another. It's simple. Natural. Like she's done it a million times. We sit like this and drink our coffee and tea in silence, and right now here in this moment, Blake is a silent calm in my personal storm.

The Morning He Fucked With The Wrong Girl

"I'm a sinner, I'm a saint
I do not feel ashamed"
-Meredith Brooks

Blake

As I walk down the long white hallways winding through the hospital, they feel like a comforting embrace, a cleanse of the inner turmoil I have been experiencing since reconnecting with Luke. I found a much needed reprieve in the silence with him. I know he needed comfort, but really, he was comforting me. He's my friend, a connection that has meant more to me, on a more meaningful level than I ever realized. A friendship I want to pursue, even though we will never materialize into something more. Even if he is more than a friend to me, more than just April's big brother who I have a crush on. So much more.

I know the only way forward with our friendship is to loop in April. I have to be honest with her, because Luke and I cannot build a friendship based on lies. Plus, I can't lie to her. She's my oldest friend. I'll see if he wants to get dinner and talk about how to go about it, decide how to bring this up to her. I grab my phone and send a text to him.

> **Me:** Do you work Saturday night?

> **Luke:** Miss me already?

> **Me:** Want to get dinner?

> **Luke:** Burgers at 7?

> **Me:** Perfect!

A smile spreads across my face and just as quickly as it appears, my blood runs cold, and the smile is gone as I recognize the body walking towards me.

"What? What do you want?" I bark out in a bitter tone as Cash approaches.

"I saw you with Luke in the Cafeteria." His reply is equally chilling.

I just stare at him, deciding acknowledging the obvious is not worth my time. I turn and walk away when he steps in my path.

"Does he know we hooked up?"

"Fuck off, Cash," I mutter in distaste, continuing to move past him.

"You're wasting your time with him. You know that right? Luke is not a guy who does no-strings arrangements. He's the type of guy who's looking for a wife,

Blake. He wants someone he can take home to mom, and spend holidays with."

His words sting, but I don't let him see the way they penetrate the armor I've built around myself.

"Good thing I've already been all those things to him. I know his mama well," I point out, pushing into him. "And we've spent many holidays together. Don't you dare try to tell me a goddamn thing about Lucas Jennings!" I seethe, "I know my fucking worth, Cash. I'm very comfortable in my skin, and confidence is not something I'm lacking. So, adjust your bruised ego and move the fuck on." This time I push past him and don't stop until I get to my car.

The cool air invades my senses as I make my way through the parking lot, each breath a welcome reset. When I close the door to my car and find myself alone in the comfort of my space, I laugh. What the fuck did I ever see in him? A pretty face and the desire to have a love that can withstand any obstacle clearly clouded me. There is no way in hell I will ever let someone like Cash diminish my self worth. I pull out of the lot, leaving behind the weight of it all, setting my sights on the road ahead-one leading to the people who truly matter and my first day off work in longer than I can remember.

Finding New Treasures

"This feeling's got me weak in the knees"
-Mandy Moore

Blake

"B," HE MOANS AS *he laces his fingers into my hair.* "*Fuck, baby. Your mouth feels incredible.*"

The view from my knees looking up at Luke's toned body, arms covered in intricate ink, is making my core ache. I feel the heat building between my legs as I take him deeper into my throat, hollowing out my cheeks and sucking in slightly.

He curls his fingers, dancing them across the back of my head as his grip tightens and he holds on as he fucks my face with rapid thrusts. He pulls out just enough for me to catch my breath as tears trail down my cheeks. With one hand I wipe them away, and I look up to meet his whisky gaze.

But when I wipe my eyes a second time, he disappears. My sight is blurred by the sun shining through the curtains in my room, and it slams me into reality.

"Fuck, I have to stop dreaming about him like that," I scold myself as I drag my ass out of bed.

I wander over to the bathroom and splash cold water on my face, trying to cool off.

I'm not sure what Luke actually looks like naked, I'm not even sure how far up his arms the ink decorating them travels, but if the real life view is even half of what my imagination conjures up in my sleep, he is one blessed man.

A few cold splashes on my face have done nothing to calm the wake of desire forging inside me after that dream, but food is number one on my list before I retreat to the shower to wash away the sweat formed by the heat of my imaginary rendezvous.

I walk over to the fridge and pull out a jar of overnight oats and pour a glass of iced coffee I've had brewing in the fridge.

I watch the cream swirl around mixing with the coffee, making intricate designs as the two colors become one. They mix with the same deliberate intensity Luke and I did in my dream.

"Damn it, Blake," I scold myself for the second time since I woke up.

Silence is a clear enemy this morning, I clearly can't be trusted in the company of my own thoughts, sneaky little suckers.

I hit play on my playlist and dance around the kitchen in my t-shirt and socks singing at the top of my lungs as I casually take bites of my overnight oats. When paired with iced coffee, it makes the perfect breakfast for a wandering soul like me who can't be bothered with little things like quickly eating breakfast or drinking a cup of coffee before they go cold. It's better when they start cold, and stay that way.

After about an hour of dancing around and exercising my toddler-like eating tendencies, I decided to hop in the shower and get ready for the day.

I don't get many days off work but when I do, having no agenda is the best agenda.

The best part of not having an agenda is allowing myself one more day before I wash my hair. It might possibly be one of my least favorite things to do, so after I'm dressed, I throw on a baseball hat and head out the door.

With nowhere to go, I've got nothing but time. There is a beautiful park not too far from my apartment with walking trails that lay beneath a canopy of maple trees, and the best part is the cutest little shopping district is right on the other side.

As I walk down the path, I can't help but admire the serenity of the scene before me. The park is full today, with families out on morning strolls, various spontaneous games taking place in the field, and dogs sniffing everything they pass. I love the bustle, especially when it's punctuated by the melody echoing in my earbuds.

About 3 songs into my playlist, I reach the shops and stop to look around, deciding where I will indulge in my guilty pleasure first, aimlessly shopping for things I don't need.

Oh, that's the perfect place, I think to myself as I walk towards my favorite thrift store. There is absolutely nothing better than a thrift store, or a good garage sale, for that matter. I love breathing new life into a forgotten treasure. Repurposing old items and making them into something spectacular.

I walk through the front door and breathe in the familiar mustiness of old fabrics, paper, and worn leather mingling with traces of past perfumes and colognes lingering on the secondhand clothing. It's a scent that tells a thousand untold stories, inviting me to uncover all the new-to-me treasures.

I head straight for the book section, hoping I can find a beautiful romance with a majestic man with long locks dancing in the wind to add to my collection.

I'm lost in the sights of my one true love when a large arm reaches around me and grabs a book off of the shelf right in front of me.

I raise my brow, irritation crossing my face. "Excuse you."

"You really get lost in the pages, don't you, B?"

Luke

I saw Blake walking across the street with her ear buds looking around like she just stepped into her own perfect little haven, happiness filling her expression. I couldn't help myself; I followed her into the thrift store and admired her as I pursued the shelves.

Blake walked through the doors, and it was like watching the weight of the world lift from her shoulders. The tension she carries melted away as she took in the space, focusing on the well, worn books stacked in uneven piles adorning the shelves.

I walked up behind her, needing to be close to her, in her space, and reached around her for any book that would grab her attention.

"Excuse you," she scolded.

"You really get lost in the pages, don't you, B?"

She spins around and looks at me, the sarcastic tone in her voice replaced by one more gentle, almost affectionate, as if she couldn't help but let her guard down.

"What are you doing?" she asks.

"Just killing time before I head home. I got called in early this morning, and if I go home right now, my sleep schedule will be all messed up," I explain.

"Do you want to join me?" Her tone is light and friendly, but her eyes give her away, she's hoping I'll say yes. Little does she know, there is no other answer.

"What are we looking for?"

"Whatever obscure treasure catches our attention."

"Junk shopping," I confirm.

"None of this is junk. It just needs the right home so it can flourish," she corrects.

"Really? Are you sure about that?" I ask as I hold up a half broken VHS tape of a 1980s workout routine, complete with a sun-faded cover and a lingering smell of mildew. "No, you're right, B, this is truly a treasure."

"Leave it to your sarcastic ass to literally pick up the one item in this store that is broken and seemingly useless."

I just laugh.

"Why are you here if you hate thrifting?"

"I don't hate thrifting, I just like giving you shit. You get all red and embarrassed."

"Let's see what else they have," she suggests, not acknowledging my teasing as she walks towards a cluster of shelves.

We walk around the store, each picking up random items to inspect them.

"Oh, look." She smiles holding up a case of old mason jars. "I can use these for literally so many things."

"So many things? They hold liquid." Confusion crosses my face. "How many things can you do with a mason jar?"

"You are such a man. You can use them as cups, DIY candle holders, I could put makeup brushes in them, use them as vases, or in my pantry to store things-so many things, Luke."

"Doesn't all the food in your pantry come in a container or bag to store them in?" Her response didn't clear my confusion, but instead caused more.

"Luke," she laughs, "You are such a man!"

"Obviously. I'm not sure why you keep saying that."

"Women like things like the pantry to be inviting, and aesthetically pleasing," she tries to explain.

"Inviting? Who are you inviting into your pantry, B? And, why would it need to be aesthetically pleasing? All you do is open the door, grab a snack, and close it. Never in my life have I opened a pantry door and thought: *this pudding cup sure would taste better if it was more appealing to the eye in here,*" I tease.

"Luke," she laughs again, and it's a sound I could listen to all day.

"I know, I'm such a man." I wrap my arm around her shoulders and pull her into a playful side hug. "What else can we get to make your aesthetics pleasing?"

"These frames are beautiful," she says when we turn down the next aisle.

"They are missing the glass," I point out.

"I can replace the cardboard back with wood and turn them into decorative trays to put on my ottoman."

I give her a sideways glance, judgement clear across my face.

"What now?" She rolls her eyes.

"You're going to buy frames and replace the cardboard backs with wood that you have to go to a hardware store to buy, find tools to use to cut it down to size so you can repurpose these frames into trays for your ottoman?" I question.

"Yes."

"Why don't you just buy these?" I ask as I raise two wood trays up for her to see.

"OH. MY. GOD. I am never going thrifting with you again." She laughs as she sets the frames down and walks to the register, mason jars in hand.

I can't help but grin, watching her fume and smile at the same time. "What, are you *sure*?" I tease. "I thought you were having fun."

"Fun?" She spins around, her eyes wide. "I don't know what you consider fun,"

I just shrug, unfazed. "You sure are laughing a lot for someone that claims this isn't fun."

She rolls her eyes, but the hint of laughter in her voice tells me there is nowhere else she'd rather be. "I swear, next time I'm leaving you in the car."

I smirk, "Next time?"

With one last dramatic sigh, she grabs her bags and heads for the door. "I'm serious. Never again."

"Sure," I say with a wink. "I'll see you Saturday."

She shakes her head but doesn't say a word.

I can't wait for next time.

Confessions Are a Bitch

"You're the closest to heaven that I'll ever be"
-The Goo Goo Dolls

Blake

Butterflies erupt in my stomach as I read the text from Luke.

There was a palpable shift between us the other day at the hospital, and then we had so much fun when we ran into each other at the thrift store, that I don't really know how to move forward from here.

The butterflies are fleeting, quickly replaced as my stomach turns into knots, guilt completely consuming me. I have to talk to April.

Luke and I are flirting with the line drawn between us every time we're together, getting dangerously close to crossing said line, and she needs to know what's going on before something happens we can't take back and it blows up in our faces.

> **Me:** I would love to! But we have to tell April.

> **Luke:** Tell her what, exactly?

Shit, he thinks I'm crazy.

> **Me:** That we're spending time together… without her. You know if she finds out before one of us tells her, she will lose her shit. She has very little cool, Luke.

> **Luke:** ☒You're right, she's a brat. I'll mention it to her tonight.

> **Me:** I did not say she was a brat! What's the occasion? It's been a while since your mom has invited me to dinner.

Luke: No occasion. I already told mom I ran into you, and she probably just misses you. Stop making this a thing.

The flutter in my chest from reading his text is now replaced by a heavy feeling. I'm so fucking stupid. To him, I'm just his little sister's friend. I have to stop making it seem like it's more than it really is when he keeps telling me it's not.

Me: See you tonight.

I pick up the phone and dial Maggie's number. It rings a few times before she answers.

"B, I'm so glad you called. Please tell me you are coming over tonight." I can hear the smile in her voice.

"I wouldn't miss it."

"Oh, good. It's been too long since I've had all three of you home." You can hear the pure joy in her response.

Home. The Jennings' house was the closest thing I have to a childhood home, at least through my high school years. But, I've convinced myself those are all the memories of my "childhood" I need, happy ones, who cares if they only date back to 14.

I imagine the warmth coming over me is a natural reaction people have to going back home after a while away.

"I can't wait, Maggie. See you tonight," I confirm before hanging up.

I spent the rest of the day doing anything and everything to distract myself from the feelings I have swirling around inside me for Luke.

I've spent almost 6 hours working on ideas for my bar. My last shift was a fucking nightmare; nothing like a toxic work environment to light a fire under my ass to get started on this.

After I put my laptop on the charger, I move to my closet to get ready. I decide it's best to go with a more "natural" appearance tonight. There is no need to look like I'm going out when I'm just hanging with family. I opt for leggings and an oversized t-shirt big enough to hang off the shoulder, long socks and my fur lined clogs. After I throw my hair up in a high ponytail, I pull a few pieces out around my face, and top it off with a shiny lip gloss instead of my usual red lip. Aiming for comfort, I even take out my contacts and put my glasses on instead. It's spring in Vermont, and the air has a cool bite to it at night, so I grab a cardigan to throw on if it gets too cold.

The drive to the Jenning's house is longer than I prefer to travel, but the scenery makes it all worth it.

There are maple trees in full bloom lining the road leading into their neighborhood, and every house seems to be adorned with tulips and irises. Their house is about 45 minutes from Cedar Creek where I live, and it looks like a different world with rolling hills, natural plush flowerbeds, and maple trees as far as you can see.

I pull into the driveway just behind April, and my shoulders tense almost immediately, knowing this might not go well.

Ignoring the tightening sensation in my chest, I hop out of my car and make my way towards her and her little teal bug that adorably fits her bubbly personality.

April and I could not be more opposite. While we are both flirtatious, she has a much louder demeanor than I do. She has a stereotypical highschool experience. She was a cheerleader who brought high energy everywhere she went, was homecoming and prom queen, and made friends easily, while I spent my nights studying at the library. We were a picture perfect cliche.

Lately, our schedules are so busy and I miss her so much when weeks go by without seeing her. We grew apart during college, but we reconnected when she moved not too far from me, and love being able to meet up more often.

My favorite is when Ana comes too, and I can spend time with both of my best friends together in the same place, even though I can tell Ana can only take April in small doses, she still makes it work for me, just one of the many reasons I love her.

"Oh, my gosh! I am so happy to see you, B! Mom said you were coming." She embraces me in the biggest hug. "Oh, Luke just moved back, so he'll be here too. Actually, he works at the hospital right by the bar now."

"I know. We actually ran into each other at the bookstore and went to dinner," I confess, thinking it's best to loop her in now since she brought it up.

"Like a date?" She scrunches her face.

"Not a date. We were just catching up."

"That's good. You know he's coming off a messy divorce, and he needs stability and predictability right now," she doesn't elaborate as she turns towards the door.

"What the hell does that mean?" I ask with frustration lacing my voice.

"Nothing." She continues to walk, and I reach out and grab her arm.

"April, you don't just say things like that without mea–"

I'm interrupted by the sound of Luke closing his car door behind me.

"Look, my two favorite girls in one place," he admires as he approaches. April rolls her eyes at me and walks inside, closing the door behind her.

Does she think I'm just trying to hook up with her brother?

"What's wrong with her?" Luke asks.

"She mentioned you were coming over tonight because you moved back. I told her I ran into you at the bookstore and we went to dinner. She asked if it was a date, and when I told her no, she seemed relieved because you're 'coming off a messy divorce and need stability.'"

"What does that mean?" he asks, his brows furrowed

"I asked the same thing, and then you pulled up, so I don't know, but it felt like she thinks I'm not good enough for you. Good thing we're not dating." I roll my eyes.

"Blake, trust me, you are more than good enough for me." He leans in and whispers in my ear, "You have been my saving grace since I moved back. And if I was lucky enough to make you mine, shit. I'd-" He clears his throat, pulls away, and moves towards the door, shaking his head. "Forget it."

Without another word, he pulls me by the hand inside like he didn't just make my head spin with what he said to me.

We immediately sit down to eat, and it's a good thing April can talk and fill the silence so effortlessly. She is getting ready to open a bakery in town, so she has a lot to say tonight, and I could not be more proud of her.

"Mom, I found the best recipe for scones. They come out so buttery and flaky. Perfection." April punctuates her description with a chef's kiss.

"Maybe you can bring some by. Dad and I would be more than happy to be your food critiques." Maggie smiles.

"I could never turn down a pastry," Matt, April and Luke's dad, cuts in. "Especially if it's made by my little ray of sunshine," he continues.

My chest tightens. I wonder what it feels like to have a father who loves you more than life itself.

Needing to shake off the emotion erupting inside me, I take a long sip of wine.

"Red," Matt chimes in with his long-standing nick-name for me, "Maggie told me you and Luke ran into each other a few weeks ago."

"Yeah," I offer a halfhearted smile, not wanting to go into too much detail in front of April as she's clearly annoyed by the whole ordeal.

Luke senses my apprehension and takes over the conversation.

"It was funny, actually. I was looking through a book at the bookstore and she sat on me."

"I didn't sit on you," I argue, and he gives me a raise of his brow. "Ok. I sat on you, but not on purpose. I was distracted while skimming a book, and didn't see you sitting there."

Matt and Maggie chuckle, and April sips her water unamused.

"Anyway," Luke continues, "We got to chatting and we decided to 'buddy read' a book," he says with air quotes.

"What in the hell is a buddy read?" his dad questions.

"It's when two people read the same book at the same time and meet up to talk about it," April interjects with annoyance in her voice. "So, that means you've met up a few times, right?"

Her gaze shifts from annoyance to anger as she looks between us, but neither of us say anything.

"Well, I think it's nice," Maggie speaks up, giving April a pointed look.

"Yeah, I guess," April responds, and then excuses herself and walks to the restroom.

Despite the uncomfortable tension between April and I, we all continue chatting for a while after she returns. After all, a few hours with the Jennings is the family time I have been needing.

The charge between Luke and I is another story. It's been hard not to gawk, so I decide to call it an early night.

"Hey, I'm going to head home," I tell April. "Can we get coffee this week and chat? I feel like we are fighting, and I hate it."

"We are not fighting, B. I'm just upset you've been lying to me."

"I'm not lying to you, I just haven't had the chance to mention it."

"Well, we're going to lunch with Ana tomorrow, so I'll see you then," she exhales sharply and I can tell she's also not being honest.

"Ok, but that's with Ana. I guess I thought we could talk, just the two of us, but I guess not."

"I'll see you tomorrow," she responds but fails to look in my direction.

"Can't wait," I respond sarcastically. "I should go." I lean down and give her a hug, a little too frayed to engage right now.

Just as I walk into the kitchen to offer my goodbyes to Matt and Maggie, my phone dings with a text.

Luke: Meet me at the bar.

Me: It's a 45 minute drive, and it's late.

Luke: Please

Debating on what the right move is, I reluctantly agree. I know he needs someone to talk to.

Me: See you there.

The entire drive back to Cedar Creek is silent. I can't bring myself to play music, or listen to a podcast, I just need the silence. To be utterly alone with my thoughts, undistracted, except they're whirling so fast I can't focus on them either.

Luke sent me a text about 15 minutes after I left, saying he was on his way. Knowing he won't be here for a few minutes, I walk inside the bar, get a table all the way in the back of the rooftop seating area away from the crowd and noise, and nervously wait.

Luke

WHEN I PULLED UP to my parents' house and saw Blake in the driveway with April, I couldn't help but stare. I love everything about Blake's go-to look, the sexy clothes on the more revealing side, her bright red cherry lips, and dark brown eyes as they shine in the light. But fuck me. Seeing her in this understated, slouchy attire, void of makeup, with her glasses on, fuck! What I wouldn't give to see what she looks like after a long night tangled in the sheets, with the sun peaking through the windows. I bet she is a vision in the morning glow.

I was so overtaken by her, I almost lost all control, words falling from my lips the second I got out of my car before I could stop them. The rest of the night, however, was full of tension after April learned we had been hanging out. Since my feelings for her almost slipped, and once I let her peek into my burning desire for her, I can't seem to turn it off, no matter what setting we are in.

So now, I'm walking into the bar to meet her, not only because I owe her an explanation, but because all I want is more time with her.

Before approaching the back corner of the rooftop where she'd texted that she had got us a table, I stopped and ordered a round of drinks. Blake is sexy and sultry, and it seems to bleed into everything in her life, including her favorite drink, apple whisky, on the rocks with a splash of ginger ale. She made it one Christmas, and I drink it often while thinking of her, so I ordered two.

As the bartender makes the drinks, I stare across the bar at Blake, watching the people around her scurry about, with a sly smile on her face. People watching is her favorite. It's one thing she loves most about her job. The incandescent string lights hung from the wood beams overhead cast a warm glow across her face, and she looks breathtaking. Each flicker cascading across her face lights up the chocolate color of her eyes, making them twinkle. The table is high, so she's propped her feet up on the foot rest at the bottom of the table, the angle highlighting the curves of her thick thighs wrapped in her leggings. Just as my eyes trail up the length of her body, my eyes meet hers, a playful smile spreading across her lips.

Fuck.

After the bartender hands me our drinks, I make my way to her, timid like a teenage boy caught with his dad's Playboys. "Hey you, see something you like?" Blake teases as she takes her drink.

"Obviously," I respond, deciding it's time to be candid about my feelings, skirting around them is becoming not only exhausting, but impossible at this point.

"Have a thing for oversized shirts and slipper shoes?" She laughs.

"I have a thing for thick thighs in leggings," I declare with a smirk, "and when they're attached to the redhead sitting across from me, they entice me even more."

She takes a long sip of her drink and then exhales. "Let's cut the shit Luke, why did you ask me here?"

"I made shit uncomfortable today," I exhale as well.

"You sure as hell did." She has nothing else to add, she just takes another pull of her drink.

"Should we just get to it, then? Address the elephant in the room," I ask.

"There's no elephant, Luke. Obviously, we're attracted to each other, but you're April's brother, and she would never speak to me again if I had a one-night stand with you."

I scoot closer and lower my voice, wanting my words to be for only her to hear. "Blake, I am extremely fucking attracted to you, but for me, it is so much more than your looks. It's everything about you." I want to be sure my intentions are crystal clear, "I love your confidence, how sexy you are in anything, anywhere. The way you bite your lip when you're thinking hard, and how you paint them red. But even more, I fucking love the way you puff your chest out when you're mad, the way you wrap your arms around yourself when you get upset, as if you're comforting yourself, your ambition, your get-shit-done attitude, and the fact you don't take anyone's shit."

"Luke," she cuts in.

"I'm not fucking done," I say with a bit of a warning in my voice. I take her hand in mine and shake my head, trying to reassemble my jumbled thoughts. "Fuck Blake, everything about you gets me going. But, most of all, it's the slight hint of honey and vanilla as it invades my senses when you're around. I want to bury myself in your scent."

My cock stirs. As I reach over and place my hand on her thigh, I feel her shift slightly beneath my touch, her muscles tighten.

"My feelings for you have been building for years, five if you want to put a fine point on it. I'll be honest, Blake, it was part of what ended my marriage. A husband should love his wife unconditionally and worship her. Instead, I found myself on more than one occasion left with the aching feeling in my gut, she wasn't you. So stop fucking downplaying what you mean to me, B. I'm not some douchebag looking to get my dick wet. I know you have had your fair share of one-night stands, and to be honest, your blatant love for sex is hot as hell, and one of the many things I love about you. I know everything about you and I know your fucking worth. So, I'm going to finish what I tried to tell you at my parents' house."

I pause waiting to see if she will let me finish. To my surprise she doesn't try to dodge the conversation, she looks at me, wanting me to continue. "If I were lucky enough to make you mine, you'd be mine forever, B. I wouldn't just fuck you one night, I'd fuck you, and worship you every fucking night for the rest of my goddamn life." I sit back and adjust my cock as it's pushing hard against my zipper, not caring if she sees what she does to me.

She swallows and opens her mouth to speak, but then takes a drink before she starts, "You were with her for a long time, Luke. You don't stay with someone for that long if you don't love them."

She's deflecting, and I'm not sure where her confidence went that I'm used to, but I don't fucking like it.

"Blake, I've had a thing for you for a long time. You are special, and when you and April came home for Christmas, right after you turned 21, everything changed for me. You walked in, and it had been a while since I had seen you, and, Blake, you took my breath away. My marriage was already in shambles, so I chalked it up to a harmless crush, a craving for the connection I was missing in my marriage, and I forced myself to forget you."

I empty my glass, needing the courage to continue. I'm already in too deep to back off now.

"I went home and tried to focus on Noel, but unfortunately in our line of work, time passes faster than you realize. We were each so busy trying to make a name for ourselves, and throughout that she turned cold. I know it sounds like an excuse, but we grew apart. We worked opposite shifts, and before I knew it we were in marriage counseling, I moved out, and then back in. It took me years to admit it was over. We'd been together for so long, it was just comfortable and predictable, and I didn't know how to leave. I thought about you often, but assumed it was only because I was missing something so vital in my marriage."

She looks away, and I reach out for her hand to redirect her attention to me.

"Then I came home one night after getting sick at work and walked in on her fucking a resident in our bed. I wasn't even mad, the opposite actually. I was relieved. When I saw her with him, the only thing going through my head was you. I was finally free from the shackles of my loveless marriage. We both deserved more than we could give each other. I tried to stay there, I really did. Noel and I actually worked better together after the divorce, but I decided I needed to be here."

"So, you came here for *me*?" she asks skeptically. " I thought you said you couldn't bear seeing her everyday."

"No, I came here because I needed my family after I got divorced, and I didn't want to be around her. We had history, and it was hard, but I hoped I'd see you. There are a lot of fucking hospitals closer to my family, Blake, but being 45 minutes away from them is still a hell of a lot closer than Denver. It's not a coincidence I work at the one across the street from the bar you work at," I answer honestly.

"Stalker! You did come here for me," she laughs, taking another drink of the amber liquid filling her glass. When she sets the glass down on the table, her eyes meet mine with a soft look, the brightness usually there, dimmed like a fading twilight, and then she continues, "Luke, why are you telling me this? Why now?"

"It feels like the right time."

She swallows, and then she bites her goddam lip. I quickly reach out and push my finger against the skin below her lip, gently pulling her lip from her teeth. "Don't fucking do that, Blake."

"Luke, I'm kind of off the market right now."

I quickly pull my hand away from her. "You're seeing someone?" I ask, confused. I haven't seen her with anyone. She hasn't mentioned anyone.

"No," she clarifies, and after a long exhale, she continues, "Luke, I know Cash." I know my face looks puzzled. "My friend Ana married his old college teammate, Knox. I've told you about Knox."

"Yeah," I respond, still confused.

"I told you I was a bridesmaid in their wedding, well Cash was there as a guest. We hooked up, and he was a total prick about it. I thought we made a connection, but he left abruptly and the next morning he was in a booth behind me in the restaurant, and… Well… he just thought I wasn't worth the effort, *not game day material.*" She pauses.

"What the hell does that mean?" He sounds like way more of a prick than he lets on.

"Who knows, probably some baseball euphemism for girls who aren't good enough. I'm not exactly sure what I expected after a one-night stand."

"One-night stands are pretty common, B, and since when do you shame yourself?" I ask, my blood boiling beneath my skin.

"It wasn't just that night; when he ended up being part of the group that was camping, he begged me not to say anything and I brushed him off. I guess it pissed him off, because when I came to see you at the hospital I ran into him in the hallway and he was a real ass. The second he saw me he said I was a fucking bitch."

My anger builds towards a guy I thought I liked, before he made my girl feel like shit.

My girl. Only she's not my girl.

"After we hooked up I did a lot of reflection, and I have to change, you know? If I want a relationship, I can't be the one-night stand girl. I'm taking a break from men so I can work on myself." She won't look at me, she just swirls her glass in her hand, watching the amber liquid swirl within its walls.

I imagine it mirroring her inner turmoil. Rage fucking boils inside me. Look at what he did to her! He touched her, was inside her, and treated her like anything other than fucking gold. I could fucking kill him.

"Blake, look at me," I coax, using my index finger to pull her chin up so her eyes are on mine. Trying to soften my tone, I take three quick breaths. "He's a fucking fool," I breathe. "Like I said before, having fun and fooling around isn't uncommon, and definitely not something you should be ashamed of. Men do it all the time, and don't slut shame themselves, and neither should you. There is nothing wrong with knowing what you like and taking it. Fuck, I might fucking kill him for doing this to you, making you feel this way," I snarl as I stand from the table.

"Luke," she demands, pulling me back down. "Sit down. No need to go all cavemen on his ass. This isn't a rescue mission."

"Look what he did to you, Blake. He made you think you are anything but perfect, not worthy of a relationship. Fuck. That. You are fucking perfect, and if anything, I can't think of a fucking guy out there truly worthy of your time."

"Not even you?" she asks, laughing.

I take a grounding breath, allowing the surrounding noises to quiet the anger building inside me. "Even me," I tell her honestly. "But I'd spend my whole life showing you I could be." I finish the water next to my empty drink in one gulp, and walk to the bar to order us another round, wondering how the fuck we move past this night of built up confessions, and where the hell we go from here.

Perfectly Flawed

"Candlelight and soul forever,
a dream of you and me together…"
-Spice Girls

Blake

Last night, Luke and I left the bar shortly after he stormed off to get us another round. We sat in a comfortable, yet tension filled silence, both of us unsure what to do with the truths we just hurled at each other. Truths echoing in the silence surrounding me, making my shoulders tense and anxiety build after an already restless night's sleep.

When he walked me to my car I could tell he wanted more. Maybe to say more, maybe to do more, but instead he stared into my eyes, brushed my cheek with his knuckle and offered a little wiggle of my chin, before smiling and opening my door.

I climbed inside, and he gently closed the door, letting the unspoken words vanish in the wind as I drove home.

This morning, the 16 year old girl with a shameless crush on her best friend's brother makes a cameo.

Luke's pissed at Cash, I know that much. While I should be worried he might do something he'll regret, all

I can think of is the fact he wants me. My stomach flips again at the thought.

I've been sitting on my couch for an hour pretending to drink my coffee. I'm snapped out of the tsunami of thoughts whirling around in my head when my doorbell rings.

The girls must be early.

Before opening the door, I set my now-cold coffee on the counter, only to come face to face with a disheveled Luke.

The door barely opened before he crashed into me.

"Luke, what are you doing? Your sister will be here soon, I think. I'm not even really sure what time it is."

He ignores the warning, as if it never left my lips, and I do the same, falling victim to the one thing I have always wanted.

I commit every motion to memory, as if time slowed, when in reality everything is unfolding in a rapid blur.

Our first point of contact is his right hand wrapping around my jaw, pulling me into a kiss. My attention quickly drifts to the veins peeking out from below the dark ink of his tattoos, only to be stolen away by a kiss, fast and urgent, yet tender. His lips envelope mine in sensual movements, and when his tongue parts my lips, I melt. His beard is rough on my skin, and fuck, I love it. He pushes me into my apartment and kicks the door closed behind him.

Fuck, it's just as hot as it is in the movies.

As he moves us farther into the apartment, he takes one hand and snakes it around my thigh, scooping me up to wrap my leg around his waist, the other leg following on its own accord. I knew Lucas was strong, but the way he just picked me up with one arm like it was nothing has me soaking through my panties already, I'm sure of it.

"Cash doesn't get to be the one who changes your life, do you hear me?" he announces, slowing our kiss, his lips never leaving mine.

"Ok," I gasp, struggling to catch my breath.

"He's not the last fucking guy who touches you, I am. But *that* mother fucker will be the last one who hurts you," he states with conviction, quickening his pace.

"Ok," I yank him into me for another heated kiss.

"You're mine, B. You are fucking mine. Do you hear me?" he commands.

"Yes," I pant.

"Say it, B. If you want me, say it."

"I'm yours. I've only ever wanted to be yours," I respond as he positions me down on my bed.

"Good! Now be a good fucking girl and get out the toy you had in the woods," he orders as he reaches his arm over his head and peels his white t-shirt off with one fluid motion.

Oh, now that's hot.

I follow his instructions, and lean over to my night-stand drawer and retrieve the toy in question. When I look up at him, I pause, taking in the sight before me. He is standing in nothing but his jeans, every ripple of his abs reflecting the light as it flutters through the window. The ink that does indeed go from wrist to shoulder, illuminated.

Luke is in my room, half naked, for me and the sight is fucking delicious.

The thought pulls my attention to the giant bulge in his pants, pressing hard against his zipper.

"Take your fucking shirt off B. As much as I want to undress you myself, I don't want to miss a fucking thing. I want to see every fucking part of you," he demands.

"What happened to mister nice guy?" I chuckle as I look down at the oversized t-shirt I am wearing. Knowing other than my panties, it's the only thing I have on.

"Baby, there is nothing nice about the things I am going to do to you." My arousal pools in my panties.

"I've been waiting too fucking long to touch you. I promise I will take my time and worship every fucking inch of you eventually, but not today, baby. Today, I need you, B. Today is about satisfying a craving."

I peel my shirt off as he stalks towards me and pulls me in one swift movement to the end of the bed. Snaking his hands behind my knees, he pulls them up so my feet are flat against the mattress. In smooth, calculated movements, he then takes one hand and pushes my knees apart so I'm spread wide open for him, all while using his other hand to pick up my toy. With the flick of a button, it is pulsing in his large hand. He scrolls through the settings before he settles on one.

"What does this do, B?" he asks, inspecting the movements.

"It… um…" I swallow, my mouth suddenly dry. "The curved side goes inside. It massages my g-spot, and the open part, it… um… wraps around my clit and sucks. It's supposed to simulate oral, when I'm alone," I respond with bated breath.

"Is that what you like? Oral?" he asks, bringing the toy to my clit and running it over my panties.

"Fuck," I moan.

"Answer my question, B," he teases, pulling the toy away.

"Yes, I love it," I answer.

He returns the vibrating end to my panties and runs it in slow circles over my clit as he leans down and whispers in my ear.

"Let's see how much you like it." In one slow sensual motion, he pulls both of my legs flat to the bed and then glides his hands with a feather like touch up the length of my legs. He softly slides my panties down, peeling them from my legs and drops them on the floor next to my bed.

He returns his gaze to me, his voice is a low gravel when he speaks, "Holy shit, your pussy is even more beautiful than I imagined, it's dripping, B." He takes the tip of his index finger and slides it between my lips, collecting the warm liquid on his finger and brings it to his mouth. When his lips close around the tip of his finger his eyes roll and a growl escapes him.

I shudder a breath in response. He leans down and returns the vibrator to my clit, circling it one time before sliding it inside. Just as it slides inside, the other part latches onto my clit and sucks hard.

"Oh, fuck," I moan, the sensation amplified by the idea of Luke watching me. I writhe and pull at the blankets and pillows around me, unable to control my hands as the tension builds. Luke's lips are on mine, with the faint taste of me on his kiss. Before I know it, he moves, trailing kisses down my body. Stopping at my nipples, he lightly sucks on each one before returning to my lips. As his mouth meets mine, he slides the toy out of my pussy and throws it hard against the wall, breaking it into pieces on contact. My eyes widen as part of it continues to vibrate on the floor.

"You're not going to fucking need to depend on this ever again," he insists breathlessly over the vibrations echoing in the air.

"No, what... Luke!" I growl out in frustration.

"I warned you I wouldn't be nice." He gives me a devilish smirk.

"I don't like being teased, Luke."

"Oh, yeah? Let's see about that," he scoffs playfully as he bends down, peppering slow sensual kisses along my torso, then down one leg, and up the other, getting just close enough to my clit I feel his broken breaths whisper over it as he passes. He kisses me everywhere, except where I want him, where I need the pressure.

"Luke, please," I beg.

"Please what, baby?"

"Please touch me."

Luke doesn't even respond. He takes one hand and drags a finger through my slit and then circles my clit with the lightest feather of a touch. He repeats this several times, before bringing his finger to his lips and sliding it into his mouth, repeating the sensual act.

"Fuck baby, you taste so fucking good," he moans.

I lay my head back against the pillow as he continues to kiss every inch of my body, savoring every minute.

Luke

I LEFT THE BAR last night haunted by the image of her face when she was talking about not being worthy of a relationship. Every time I closed my eyes, I saw hers glistening with unshed tears, a shimmer with a muted glow replacing their usual bright sparkle. It made me want to fucking kill Cash.

I decided then and there I was done fucking around. She is worthy of more love than anyone could give, and she will have it. I'm done letting my doubts and wants clank against each other like balls swinging on a pendulum. She deserves to be fucking worshiped, and over my dead fucking body will anyone else get the mother fucking chance to do it.

Letting go of everything holding me back was a freeing feeling I have never experienced, but right now in this moment, it's no match for my lips on her body. The curves of her hips, the thickness of her thighs, the perfect size of her breasts filling my palm. Fuck! Nothing will ever match this.

I trail kisses up and down her body, purposely avoiding the place I know she wants me. She already said it was her favorite. I love watching her writhing with want, desperate for me, for *my* touch.

She's not the only one losing patience, so I decide to end the charades. I work my way down her body, the smell of her arousal engulfing my senses. Taking my fingers, I spread the lips of her pussy so I can see her clit, swollen and needy. With careful precision, I run my tongue across the sensitive area, circling it before going back and adding more pressure, this time adding one finger and curling it upward to massage the exact spot I imagine her toy awoke before.

"Fuck, Luke!" she pants and I lose control.

I pick up my pace as the tension builds, her legs forming a tight restraint around my head, her wet cunt coating my beard as I eat her up. The best fucking prison I could imagine. Just as her toes curl and her breathing becomes erratic, I quickly pull away and fumble with the button on my jeans.

"Shit, I'm going to fucking kill you!" she stammers.

"Baby, you're about to come, and I'm about to have an embarrassing show in my pants if I don't get inside you right fucking now. If I'm going to make you come for the first time, you're going to come all over my dick," I instruct firmly as I retrieve a condom from my wallet. I place it between my teeth and tear the package open, and as I hear giggles from the bed. "Is my dick funny?" I have to ask, my ego a little bruised by the response.

"Fuck no! Your dick is fucking huge and I love it. I'm honestly a little scared it won't fit, but how in the hell do you make everything look so damn sexy?" she laughs.

"Laughing like that is only going to get you spanked, B."

"Sorry, but Lucas fucking Jennings is standing in front of me naked, and is hard for *me*." Her laugh tapers off when I climb on top of her and line myself up with her entrance.

"Baby, I can promise you this is not the first time I've been hard for you."

As I slide in, she gasps, "Luke, it's too big."

"Does it hurt?" I ask, pulling back.

"No, I'm just afraid it will." She shifts with uncertainty.

"I would never fucking hurt you, B. I promise I'm made for you. I'll fit perfectly. I'll go slow."

"No, I'm ready. I don't want you to go slow. You promised you wouldn't be nice, Luke."

With a soft submission, I watch her succumb to the pleasure as I wrap my hand around her throat and kiss her delicate lips. She purrs as my fingers wrap around her throat. The sight is pure perfection as my dick slides inside. The walls of her cunt pulsing slightly with each inch as I enter her.

"Baby, relax. You're so tight." She laughs at my request and her walls clench tighter. "Fuck. Don't do that! I want to last at least a few seconds," I beg.

I pump in and out of her, holding my hand with a steady grip around her throat, careful not to apply too much pressure to her windpipe, but just enough to her carotid to slow the blood to her brain, intensifying the sensation between her legs, picking up the pace with each thrust. She digs her nails into my back and drags them down my skin, as I feel her body shudder beneath me. I'm sure there will be marks for days. When I loosen my grip after a few seconds, she places her hand over mine, signaling for me to tighten it again. I follow her silent request, and feel the walls of her wet pussy tightening around me.

My girl likes it a little rough.

"It's not time for that baby, we're just getting started."

Needing to listen to myself, I slowly pull out of her.

"What-"

I answer her question with a flick of my tongue over her swollen clit.

"Luke," she moans.

I circle her clit one more time, before sliding my tongue along her opening. I spread her open with two fingers and marvel at the slick coat of her arousal glistening off the pink flush of her cunt. It's the most beautiful sight in the world. I slide my tongue inside her, wanting a taste. Slowly eat her pussy like it's the last thing I'll ever taste, pulling her closer to me.

"Luke?" she questions.

"Yes, B?"

"I miss you inside me,"

"You're in charge, baby. Tell me how you want me."

"Get back inside me, Luke."

I move to kiss her and she silently takes control, instantly lining me back up. I prop myself on one arm next to her head on the bed and make sure the other is fully extended against so I can see every detail of her perfect face. My other hand is propped against her headboard, offering support as I pump in and out of her.

"You look so hot like that," she pants, "all propped up like a thirst trap. So fucking sexy."

"It gives me the best view around," I insist.

As my pace quickens, she wraps her legs around my waist, tightening them with each thrust. Before I know it, her body is convulsing, and her walls are tightening. They're so tight, I can feel every ridge and curve of her pussy. The thought causes me to find my own release way sooner than I wanted.

Fully sated, I collapse on top of her, barely able to breathe.

I hear my sister's voice just as the bedroom door flies open. "Bla- Oh shit, sorry! Ew, oh my god, what the fuck?" April's voice is full of disbelief as she scurries out of the door and closes it quickly.

"Fuck, fuck Luke. This is not how I wanted her to find out," Blake grits out frantically, climbing out from under me and fumbling to find her clothes.

Seconds later, Ana comes barreling in, but quickly snaps the door shut behind her and pushes against it when she sees me. "Oh…" she giggles with a hand over her eyes. "She's going to fucking kill you! No, seriously, she's going to kill you. I told you to tell her," she whispers, scolding in Blake's direction between her teeth. "Why would you have him here knowing we'd be here soon?"

"I'll go talk to her," I insist as I pull my shirt over my head. "Better if she loses her shit on me."

"I didn't know he was coming over. We didn't plan this," Blake tries to explain as I open the door.

"Luke, wait," she calls out, but before she can stop me, I'm out the door.

"April," I yell down the hallway as I approach the kitchen where my sister is sitting on the stool at the counter.

"Lu- WHAT the FUCK? You-yo-" Her words fade off.

"Listen to me ok, because I'm not fighting with you over this, April. It's no fucking secret B and I have feelings for each other, and I know I'm way fucking older than her, but-" She stands and interrupts me.

"I don't give a fuck how many years are between you. You're both fucking adults, Luke. I can't believe you were fucking my best friend and neither one of you had the fucking sense or courtesy to tell me, so I didn't have to find out by walking in on it. I even asked her last night and she lied to me."

"She didn't lie to you. Before last night, nothing was going on between us."

"So what? You just woke up and decided, *I'm going to fuck Blake today*, and showed up here?"

"No. You know me better than that."

"Do I?"

"Why are you so upset about the idea of us?" I know why she's mad about how she found out, but what I don't understand is why she's mad in general?

She lowers her voice from a yell to a very low whisper yell, "She needs someone like you, Luke, and you need anyone fucking else than Noel. Blake is the best fucking thing I could ask to happen to you, but you are coming off a fucking divorce, and she is still recovering from a bad one-night stand with Cash, and I'm not sure either of you are in a fucking place to really be what the other deserves right now," April pleads.

"April, I stayed far too long in my fucking marriage as it deteriorated around me because I wasn't the husband Noel needed. And while in the end she was the one who cheated, I was the one pinning over my little sister's best friend. I've been head over heels for her since Christmas 5 years ago. When I moved back here I took my fucking feelings for Blake and I tried to ignore them because I was a fucking coward. Well, now that I've admitted them, I can't take them back. This time around-" I lower my voice, "this fucking time around I'm doing things differently than I did with Noel, I am taking my fucking time with Blake so we can be exactly what the other needs." My voice is cracking slightly as I finish.

"I don't think either of you is in the right place to take on a relationship right now, and watching you self-destruct isn't something I want." She stands and grabs her purse just as Blake comes running out of her room.

"April, please don't leave. Please," Blake yells as she enters the main living space.

"Do you love him?" April snaps.

"We're not," Blake protests. "This is, this... kind of."

"So, he's just a hookup?" April interrupts.

I sigh and let my head fall.

April looks at me, with betrayal in her eyes. "What happened to all that 'I'm going to take my time' bullshit you just spewed?" she mocks looking back at Blake. "So, you're just fucking my brother, and you want me to do what? Be ok with you two having a fling, and just cross my fingers and hope it doesn't destroy the two most important people in my life, and hope I'm not the one who loses everything in the process?"

"I can't explain it right now," Blake's voice cracks, "He's more than that. It's just–"

April storms out of the apartment, slamming the door behind her before Blake can finish her sentence.

Sometime It's Hard Before It's Easy

"Cause it's a bitter sweet symphony, this life…"
-The Verve

Blake

I KNOW SHE DIDN'T mean to hurt me when she left, but Ana didn't say a word, just gave me a hug accompanied by an "I told you so" look. It stung, because I know she was right. I was just too stubborn to listen. April deserved to hear I had feelings for her brother from me. She deserved to hear it before anything happened.

"You said you were mine," Luke whispers, seemingly out of nowhere. "Then acted like we were nothing." He sighs and starts towards the door.

"Luke," I grab his arm and pull him into me. He turns and sinks down on the back of the couch. "You know it's not what I meant. I meant we haven't been seeing each other behind her back, like she thought we were. Look at me," I plead, placing my forehead against his. "I am yours. Always have been."

"Then you'll be my girlfriend, for real?" he asks.

"Are we in middle school?" I laugh. "I figured you fucking my brains out and me panting your name kind

161

of sealed the deal, but, fuck yes, I will be your girl-friend, Lucas Jennings."

Without a word, Luke slings me over his shoulder and carries me back to the bedroom. A shriek leaving my mouth as he slaps my ass one time hard enough to leave a mark.

"Fuck! Luke that hurt," I screech, blowing my hair out of my face.

"Don't worry, baby. I'll kiss it better," he promises as he closes my bedroom door behind us and locks it.

"We're all alone now. I'm not sure the lock is nec-essary," I tease.

"I'm not taking any fucking chances, baby." He raises a brow as he sets me down on the bed.

It's been about two weeks since April walked in on Luke and I. While Luke's parents are so excited we are dating, April seems less than thrilled. They have dinner at their parents' house every weekend, and Luke says she still isn't really talking to him unless she has to. I knew she would be mad, but I figured she'd have her dramatic moment and then just get over it. She never burdens herself with emotions about things she can't control. She prefers to be happy.

This is all I can think about as I mindlessly pour a few beers for the regulars who are sitting across the counter from me at the bar.

"Blake, what the fuck!" Harvey, my manager, yells and scares the shit out of me, beer splattering across the counter as the glass slips from my hand.

"Excuse me?" I challenge.

"The money didn't add up from your register last night. I told you to check it and make sure it was all logged correctly before you left. Are you stealing from me?" he accuses.

"First," I snap back, "I *did* check it and you signed off on it, saying I logged it correctly before you paid me out on my tips. I am tired of this shit, Harvey. You ask for help with shit, and then you do a piss-poor job of double checking the things you need to and try blaming everyone else."

"You can't talk to me like that, I'm your boss."

"So that entitles you to accuse me of stealing from you to cover for your mishap, in front of customers?" I argue.

"My mishap? I am missing money, you think I'd be freaking out if I was the one who stole it?" There is no reasoning with him.

"I would NEVER fucking steal money. You know what? Fuck this. I quit." Infuriated, I untie my apron and slam it down on the bar. He yells after me as I walk towards the door, but I don't give a shit. Harvey can kiss my ass.

Ten minutes later, I'm at Luke's door.

"Baby, what's wrong?" he asks, concern etched in his expression as he reaches for me.

I walk in, my body still blazing with adrenaline. I can feel the flush in my cheeks, as my breaths come quick and shallow, like I've just sprinted the entire way here. My hair, usually neatly tied back for work, has come loose in wisps as they cling to the sheen of sweat coating my face. I'm pacing back and forth across the main living space of Luke's apartment. My hands are moving wildly to punctuate each point as the words spill from my mouth, my voice sharp and edged with frustration. "That fucking piece of shit accused me of stealing money from him. He said the fucking cash from my register wasn't adding up from last night, after the dickweed counted and verified it in the motherfucking ledger."

"What the fuck, B. You don't need to take his shit," he snaps sharply.

"Oh, trust me, I know. I quit on the spot." Just as the words leave my mouth, realization sets in. I collapse on the couch behind me, the weight of my decision crashing into me like a tidal wave. My chest tightens and my hands tremble as the adrenaline gives way to the emptiness in the pit of my stomach. I stare down at the floor, my jaw clenching, I don't have a job anymore.

Instantly, my eyes dart around the living room, trying my hardest to avoid Luke's gaze, as if it will somehow make the truth less real. "I don't have a job," I whisper.

"I'm glad you quit, B. You are so much better than that place. You've been miserable for a long time, and it was taking a toll on you."

"Luke, I don't have a fucking job. How in the hell am I going to pay any of my bills, or my rent, without a paycheck?" I panic.

"B, this is a good thing," he reminds me, bending down and brushing the hairs from my face. "You can move in here, and save for a few months, add it to the money you have for a down payment on a place to open on your own."

"Luke, we've been together for like a second. We can't live together."

"Says who?" he asks.

I think about it for a second. "My lease isn't up for a while. I can't afford to break it," I state the obvious.

"You'll figure it out, and if you need help, I'm here, B. You're not on your own anymore"

I drop my eyes with a shy grin, unable to stop my smile as it threatens to break free, "But I don't want to rely on you for everything." I take a calming breath.

"Why not?" he asks. "If I offer to help, please, let me spoil you."

"Maybe," I whisper, feeling the weight of my lease. "But, I like my independence. I enjoy taking care of myself, Luke."

"Independence is amazing, baby, but in this case it might be like juggling flame torches, liberating but risky. Sometimes it's nice to let someone else handle the sparks so you can enjoy the heat!" he suggests. "You know what?" he continues. "Let me just show you, instead."

He lifts me off the couch and carries me to his room, peppering kisses up and down my neck as we walk.

Luke

"YOU WANT TO KNOW what every single day could be like, baby?" I whisper.

"I think I have a pretty good idea." She smiles as she takes my earlobe between her lips and sucks lightly.

"Let's not leave anything to the imagination, huh?" My infatuation with her is unwavering. I want her in my arms, in my bed, on my tongue, and wrapped around my cock every second of every day.

I lay her down on the bed and lay kisses down her neck as I unbutton the black shirt she wore to work. When the last button's unfastened, the fabric falls away from her chest, exposing the black lace bra underneath. The slight blush color of her pebbled nipples peeking through the veil of fabric. "B, this," I breathe heavily, running my knuckle over the thin lace, "This is fucking incredible. Do the panties match?"

"I don't think so, given I'm not wearing any," she taunts with a lustful smile and a wink.

"Fuck," I groan as I peel the leggings she is wearing away from her porcelain skin. Her freshly waxed pussy, glistening in the dim light of the lamp on my nightstand. "You baby, are in charge," I submit, kissing her ankle and steadily moving up.

"I want you to fuck me, leave me breathless," she moans.

"Well, that's a guarantee, but you've been holding out on me a little baby. I want you to know how good it feels to be promiscuous, a little reckless, and take exactly what you want, no shame, when it's with the right person," I whisper softly, continuing to kiss my way up her body. "Tell me what to do to you, baby girl."

"I… I don't know," she whispers.

"Need a little inspiration?" I ask.

"What?" she asks in a chuckle, lifting her head off the mattress to look at me.

"Here," I breathe out, handing her the copy of 'Evermore' I bought the day we ran into each other at the bookstore. "I dogeared several sections of the book. Pick one." She looks at me, raising a brow in question.

"B, the entire time I read this book, I pictured what it would be like to do the things I was reading to you, so I marked the pages with my favorite scenes, in case I ever got the chance," I lightly blow on her clit, and she shudders at the sensation. "Now, pick one and read it to me."

"You want me to read to you?" she asks. "Out loud?"

"Yes. You don't know what you want me to do to you, so use this to get you started. Read it to me, and I will do every fucking thing as it leaves that pretty fucking mouth of yours."

Her breath is ragged as she opens the book. She skims some of the marked pages before settling on one. *"He, He runs his-*um,*"* she reads with a cough. *"He runs his knuckles up my stomach and when he reaches each nipple, he unfolds his fingers so he circles them lazily with the pad of his fingers. Not once, not twice, but three times each."* She swallows as I do exactly as she says, my eyes intently watching her chest rise and fall with each ragged breath.

"He works his way down my body, every touch punctuated by the heat of his breath as he moves his way down my body until he reaches the sensitive skin of my soaking pussy. Just when he reaches the most sensitive parts of my body, he takes his tongue and slides it between my lips until he reaches my clit. He circles it several times before adding the most delicious pressure with his tongue." She stops reading, her eyes moving to meet mine. This causes me to pause.

"If you want me to keep going, B, you have to keep reading."

"I can't focus on the words with you between my legs," she breathes out.

"Ok," I retreat to lay back on the pillow beside her head.

"Ok? What are you doing?" she asks.

"I said you were in charge. If you can't tell me what to do, then we can go to bed," I tease lightly, turning off the light.

She takes three long breaths, each one deeper than the one before it. "Turn it back on, Luke. I can't read in the dark," she whispers.

As I reach back over and turn on the light, her voice continues on a ragged breath, *"Just when he reaches the most sensitive parts of my body, he takes his tongue and slides it between my lips until he reaches my clit. He circles it several times before adding the most delicious pressure with his tongue. Fuck Luke,"* she moans and I do exactly as the page describes. *"He then slides two fingers into my soaking pussy, reaching in as far as he can, applying pressure in an upward motion as he slides his fingers in and ou-* Fuck Luke, shit," she moans.

"I don't remember this being in the book, but fuck baby, I love the way it's making you moan my name," I speak with heat as I repeat the motion.

"Oh, fuck!" She shudders and her walls tighten around my fingers. "Fuck me, Luke."

"I don't think that's in the book, baby."

"Fuck the book. You said I was in control. Fuck me right now," she demands, flipping onto all fours. "Hard."

I stand and walk over to my nightstand when her words stop me in my tracks.

"I have an IUD, Luke. Got it after Ana found out she was pregnant with Riker. Fuck me, bare. Please. I want to feel every inch of you inside me, all of you."

Her words make my rock hard erection push even harder against my pants. As I reach down and pull my pants and boxers down, my erection springs free. Her eyes instantly make their way down my body, and when her eyes meet my dick, she softly licks her lips as she moves to the edge of the bed next to where I am standing. She reaches out her hand, wrapping it softly around my length as she takes her tongue and licks her way over my balls cupped in her other hand.

"Blake, baby," I hiss. Just as the words leave my mouth, she slides my entire length into her mouth until I feel the back of her throat, just before she goes to slide it out, her throat contracts, and I fucking see stars. "Baby," I say in a hurry trying to pull away from her, but she sucks harder, "you asked me to fuck you bare, and the thought just about made me come in my pants, so if you continue to suck my dick the way you are, I won't make it inside you."

She gives me a devilish grin as she slides me out of her mouth and climbs back on all fours, and I line myself up with her entrance. As I slide in, heat radiates around my dick, the sensation sending a shiver up my spine. I knew she'd feel amazing if I ever got to feel her bare, but my imagination doesn't hold a candle to the reality of how fucking good she actually feels. She is so wet, so smooth, so warm, and I fucking love every second of it. I pump in and out of her at a vigorous pace, while the sounds of her screams and our skin slapping fill the room. Neither one of us lasts long, quickly finding our release and when we both come down from the high, we cuddle, me still inside her, and I can't think of a better place to be right now than here in this moment with her.

I didn't want to make her feel like she had to agree to move in with me, so I waited until morning to bring it back up.

It definitely took some convincing, but today, nearly three weeks later, Blake is living in my apartment. Convincing her to live here was easy. Convincing her to let me pay to break her lease was much harder. Accepting help doesn't come easy to her, so when she suggested that she'd pay the utilities and groceries, I reluctantly gave in. Blake is stubborn and passionate, she prides herself on *"not needing anyone to rescue her."* I guess she's guarded from a life of being let down by her mom.

I walk in the door after a long shift, the sun just peeking through the curtains as it rises in the sky. I took a nap in one of the on-call rooms earlier this evening, knowing I would want nothing to do with sleep when I walked in my apartment to B in my fucking bed.

The apartment is dim and silent, prompting me to tiptoe down the hallway, each creak of the floorboards sounding like tiny fireworks with every step I take. I stroll into the bedroom and find the bed is empty. I lay my bag down just when I see Blake out of the corner of my eye, in the bathroom, curled up in the bathtub in the fetal position. "B, what's wrong? Are you hurt?" I ask, rushing to her, panic lacing my voice.

"Hey babe," she replies in a strained voice.

"Why are you sitting like someone punched you in the stomach?" I ask.

"I woke up with the worst cramps, my insides feel like they're about to fall out on the floor," she groans.

I reach behind me and pull my shirt and hoodie off in one swoop and drop my pants and boxers to the floor.

"Scoot up, baby." I nudge her forward a little.

"No, Luke, please don't I'm bleeding."

"And you're in pain, and you need your boyfriend to hold you, make you feel better," I insist and she concedes, moving forward so I can slide in behind her.

"Holy fuck!" I shout, as my foot hits the tub, hopping in a small circle trying to avoid the water.

"What? Oh God, you can see it, can't you? I knew this was a bad idea." She winces, covering her eyes and turning her head away from me.

I laugh and pull her into me as I ease myself into the water. "No, baby, it's just, this water is going to fucking boil my insides. Why the hell is it so hot?"

"It makes the cramps less intense," she replies.

"There isn't a less fucking painful way to make the pain go away?" I ask, shifting behind her.

"There are a lot of things that make it better, but this is the first thing I do, because it relaxes my muscles."

"Sounds like you have a ritual," I joke.

"When you have this shit every month, you find as many ways as possible to stop the fucking pain," she deadpans.

"Tell me how to make it better," I whisper in her ear.

"Well, if I'm home, and not working or something, I pop some pain relievers and take a hot bath. I soak for about 30 minutes until the water gets cold. Then I eat dark chocolate, and sip on some tea to help hydrate. Then I either do yoga or get out one of my toys and make myself orgasm a few times." Her tone is serious. "Then I take a nap and usually-"

"What?" I interrupt. "Back up."

Knowing exactly what I'm surprised by, she laughs, "Luke, the contractions of an orgasm make the muscles of the uterus relax or some shit. You're a doctor. Why are you so surprised by this?"

"I work on emergency injuries and trauma, not vaginas," I answer. "Wait, you knew I was coming home, so what were you going to do, get yourself off while I'm sleeping next to you?" I ask as I gently cup the water in my hands and pour it across her breasts peeking out of the water.

"Maybe." She shrugs.

"You're such a fucking tease sometimes," I place gentle bites down her neck.

"Can you hold me a little tighter?" she asks. "These cramps are more intense than usual."

I wrap my arm around her waist and pull her into me tight. Then I take my other hand and snake it around her leg, curled tight to her chest, and glide my fingers over her clit.

Her eyes wide, she tries to pull away. "Luke! No, you're-"

"Shhh," I whisper, kissing her temple. "Lay your head back and let me make you feel better. Besides, I broke that fucking toy, remember? I said you'd never need to depend on it again, and I meant it, baby." I continue laying lazy circles around her clit. She moans and the sounds echo against the tiles in the shower, a beautiful melody filling the surrounding space. I continue making circles with one hand as I use the other to support her weight as she goes limp in my arms. The tension builds in her limp body as it shakes in my grip. I apply a little more pressure over her clit and roll my finger back and forth until she comes, and just when she finishes, I gently work her clit again until a second orgasm builds, and then a third.

When she is completely satiated, I crawl out from behind her and turn on the shower. When the water is warm, I walk back over to the tub and lift her out, carrying her into the shower and placing her on the small bench, opposite the showerhead. She goes to reach for her loofah and body wash and I step in front of her reach.

"Luke, I can take care of myself," she rolls her eyes.

"I know, but you don't have to. Let me make you feel better."

"You already made me feel better," she announces with joy, looking at me all doe eyed.

Without a word, I grab her loofah and load it with her body wash. A hint of vanilla and honey fills the air, the scent I have developed a love for, and crave, enveloping us like a cozy blanket.

I slide the mesh over her skin, suds covering every inch of her. As the water runs clear of suds, I wash myself and then wrap us both in towels.

The towel around my waist hangs low as I carry her to the bed. Little soft moans escape her mouth as I lather her in lotion. Starting at her feet and making my way up her body, I am careful to add just the right amount of pressure as I rub the cream into her skin.

I place one of my t-shirts on the bed as I go to retrieve some chocolate and tea. When I get to the kitchen, I realize I don't know how she takes her tea, so I walk back to the room to ask her. When I enter the doorway to the dimly lit room, she is fast asleep on my pillow. I slide on a pair of briefs and move in behind her.

Her presence is familiar, comforting. But the closeness has a weight to it, one I know won't be easy to shake off.

Big Things are Coming

"I wanna thank you for given' me the time to breathe…"
-Christina Aguilera

Blake

I MOVED INTO LUKE'S apartment three weeks ago.

We have officially, as of last night, had sex on every surface in here. The last place being the one he has been saving. He insisted he wanted to remember the first time he fucked me there, ending our first time marathon, right smack dab in the middle of the pantry, where he could enjoy his favorite "snack." Who knew there were so many uses for gummy bears?

That's where my mind is right now, as I wait on hold with my commercial real estate agent. I'm drifting back to thoughts of Luke, nibbling the edges of various gummy bears and sticking them in a trail across my body, eating each one off me, until he got "distracted" by the body parts they were sticking to. When we finished, we were both a sweaty, sticky mess, and continued the fun in the shower.

The booming voice of Chase, my realtor, abruptly interrupted my thoughts.

"They accepted your application, but you're going to need a business loan by the weekend for the rest of the down payment!" he all but yells through the phone.

"For real? I thought they had several applications come through?" I ask, barely able to contain myself.

"The owner of the space is and I quote, 'A woman's woman.' She loved your business plan and how liberating it was going to be for women in this town," he explains. "All the other applicants were either chains or businesses that lacked the appeal you had."

"Holy shit! When can I get in to set it all up?" I ask.

"You sign in two weeks, but she said you can start scheduling contractors to come on Monday."

Owning a bar has been a dream of mine for as long as I can remember. After exploring several concepts, I went with my favorite idea: a spicy book bar. Lit and Libations will officially be open for business, soon!

Last week, Luke and I were on a walk and I noticed a little storefront in town I absolutely fell in love with. It's a few blocks from our apartment and is the perfect place to start up my small business. I think back to the day and smile.

"Luke, look at this place!" my cheeks hurt from smiling. "This is perfect. It's small, intimate. It has hardwood floors like I imagined, and the exposed bricks and the pipes give it an industrial vibe."

"It's absolutely perfect, baby. I think the best part is the storybook window in the front. It would be the perfect place to put a bench seat. I can build you one." The look in his eyes was genuine and loving.

Ever since I put in the offer, I can envision it. It all comes alive in my head: a cozy space that serves as both a spicy bookstore and a bar, blending the best of both worlds, and creating a place where people can come and truly escape the grind of day-to-day life. The warm, hardwood floors and exposed brick walls create a home away from home. Shelves lined with books will accompany cozy reading nooks scattered throughout the room, perfect for curling up with a novel and a drink. The centerpiece is a whimsical bar, round in the center, with warm lights casting a glow off the glass shelves. The air is filled with the rich aroma of spiked coffee and the subtle notes of wine floating through the air, creating the perfect setting to host a book club, get lost in a book, or socialize with other readers. A place where I can truly unleash my most exotic mixology creations.

Thankfully, the space is charming on its own, and the only real construction that needs to be done is building a bar in the center of the room. My biggest undertaking is stocking the book inventory.

With more excitement than I can contain, I pick up the phone to call Luke. I know he's at work, but he knows I've been waiting for this call.

"Hey, B," he says with a smile in his voice.

"I got it! The owner loved my business plan and said I can start sending contractors over on Monday."

"Shit! That's amazing, baby. L&L will be up and running sooner than you thought! I'm so fucking proud of you, baby."

"Right? This is like a dream. Listen, I'm going to see if Ana and April want to go get dinner and celebrate. Hopefully April will come." I sigh. "Then I'm going to pick up dessert and bring it to the hospital so I can celebrate with you."

"I can't wait, but trust me, there will be plenty of celebrating when I get home." His voice is spiked with heat.

The thought makes my knees weak. "B, I'm so proud of you," he professes one last time, before we hang up.

Phone still in hand, I type out a message to Ana and April, holding my breath as I hit send, hoping April will at least respond. After she walked in on Luke and me, she had been really standoffish. I don't blame her, I would be mad too. I tried calling her like crazy after she left. After many failed attempts, I showed up at her apartment, and made her talk to me, but there is a distance there I hate so much.

To my surprise, April responded just a few minutes before I got to the burger bar and let me know she would be here. Even after our short conversation she's still upset. I can't really blame her, it's not even the idea of us being together that's putting her in a funk. She's just worried we're going to crash and burn the second there is tension, but we are stronger, I know it.

Ana and I are already at the table when she walks in, a bright yellow bag in hand, her face impassive.

"I can't believe you did it!" Ana continues as April pulls out the chair next to me. She leans over and gives me a hug and places a soft kiss on my temple.

"It really is amazing. Tell me all about it," she urges.

I'm pleasantly surprised by her warm demeanor.

"Hey," I return the hug, though brief. "I'm glad you came. I wasn't sure you would."

"Why?" She looks at me like she hasn't the faintest idea.

"Um… you've been pissed at me and we barely speak."

"We can have our differences and still be there to support each other," she reassures me. "I'm proud as fuck of you, even though I'm mad at you. Let's not talk about it right now, though."

I nod, not wanting to ruin the night. She and I can have it out some other time. Tonight, I just want to stuff my face with burgers and celebrate with my two best friends.

We each opted for all you can eat. A love for burgers is something we all have in common.

"How did you find this place?" Ana asks, shoving fries into her mouth.

"Luke suggested it after we ran into each other at the bookstore." I wince, not wanting to make April uncomfortable.

"Don't do that," she sounds annoyed. "Either date my brother and be confident in it, or don't."

You could cut the tension with a knife, so Ana interjects just in time.

"Alright, so what are your plans for the store?" Ana interrupts, changing the subject.

My voice is unsteady as my throat constricts, fighting back the emotion building behind my words. I start off quiet, but the more I tell them all about the space, I find myself lost in the excitement, almost forgetting April's words, almost.

"I really want it to be a cozy place people can go to escape, and fall into a book after they buy it."

"That sounds amazing." Ana's attention doesn't leave mine, but mine's fixed on April. She offers me a soft smile and asks what else I have planned.

"I'm in the process of creating a drink menu with punny book names to serve at the bar.

"Ooh, what about Tequila Mockingbird?" Ana asks with a chuckle.

"No, Cheeky Chi-tini," April fires back, her voice much lighter.

"No, no, Hellcat High roller," Ana nods her head in approval. "A nod to MK. She's my favorite FMC."

We spend the next hour laughing and making grand plans for the opening.

"This made my night, you guys. Thank you for coming." I smile at them both. I know April came around, but I hate feeling uneasy around her. "Would you guys like to come help me get everything set up this weekend?"

"I can't believe you can get set up already. I mean, I know it feels like it's taking forever to you, but this is moving quickly." April's voice is cheery on the surface, but I know her well enough to hear the slightly forced undertone.

"I think the landlord is eager to have the rent covered." I smile.

"Knox and I would love to help," Ana cuts in.

"Me too, of course. I should have led with that," April adds.

Despite the lighthearted change in her demeanor, there's something in the way she's watching me, like she's reading too much into everything, and it's making the air between us heavier than it should be.

"LUKE, THIS IS AMAZING," Blake sniffles through watery eyes.

I wanted to do something nice for her to show her just how proud I am of all the hard work she's been putting in. The neon sign I ordered for her to hang behind the bar finally came in, and the designer did a better job than I could have ever imagined. Little embellishments of dark emerald green, to mimic the perfect shade of greenery she plans to scatter across the space, enhancing the bold script that reads "Lit and Libations."

"They did an amazing job," I marvel. The look in her eyes any time something arrives at the bar makes me even more glad I moved her in here, where I get to witness every single expression crossing her face. It's been a few weeks and today is the day Blake takes occupancy of the space. We decided we needed to start with assembling bookshelves so they are ready to be lined with books.

Blake came over early this morning to sign for all the deliveries. She's been ordering things like crazy in preparation for today. She's been so excited for this day, she might have been a little ambitious in her plans.

I came a few hours later when I got off work.

If I know nothing else about my girl, it's that she needs food, or "hanger" sets in and she's unbearable, so I brought breakfast also knowing she's terrible at feeding herself when she gets busy.

In just a few brief hours, all the reinforcements we called in will be here. My mom and dad, Ana and Knox, and April will be here to help unload all the book inventory onto the shelves. For now, it's just the two of us, assembling her perfect space and bringing it to life.

"Why don't you take a break for a few minutes and come drink some coffee and eat a bit? You're going to need fuel, so you have enough energy to get all of this done today," I encourage her.

"Yeah, ok, Doc," she mocks.

"Don't mock me, or I'll spank your fine ass until it's hard for you to sit," I tease.

"Oh that doesn't sound like the punishment you're intending." Her laugh is light and full of amusement.

After she finishes placing the last shelf on the case we just assembled, she stands and wipes her hands on her pant legs. As she saunters over to the bar, the smile crossing her face as she takes in the progress we have made heats my insides. She is so goddamn beautiful with her hair a mess in her ponytail, the beads of sweat gliding down her temple, and the gentle flush of pink on her cheeks, but the most amazing part of the package is the globes of her ass in the black leggings she is wearing. I want to touch her, to kiss her, to take her right here on the bar, but I know she needs to eat, and if I distract her now, she will lose all interest in her food.

I sit back and watch her take tiny little nibbles off the bagel with tiny little bits of strawberry cream cheese sticking to her lower lip. She sets down the bagel and starts taking bites of pineapple and strawberries off the fork, and my cock stirs to life. I wait patiently until the last bite of her bagel is gone before I stand and make my way over until I'm standing right behind her.

"Pink suits you," I praise, kissing her neck.

"What?" she asks, turning her stool until she is facing me.

Just as her face comes into full view, I bend down and kiss her lips, sure to suck the small bit of strawberry cream cheese off her bottom lip as I pull away.

"And fucking delicious," I whisper in her ear.

"Luke, we have so much to do," she protests as I nibble her skin and work my way from her lip to her neck to her shoulder and pull the loose fabric of her sweatshirt down, just enough to expose the skin.

"We do, but we have hours until everyone will be here, and taking breaks is essential to a positive work environment. I wouldn't want to file a complaint that you worked me to the bone with no break," I tease.

"Oh, well, I would hate to open with a complaint on record," she jokes. "Wouldn't want to work you to the bone."

"Work me to the bone, or until I have boner? I guess it's just semantics." I shrug.

"Luke," she giggles.

"Baby, nothing I am going to do to you will be safe to show on record."

"That's too bad," she sighs as she stands, pulling her leggings down in one slow, sensual motion. "I guess I'll have to erase the surveillance footage later."

"Don't you fucking dare," I bark back at her.

I walk over and rub my hand up the inside of her thigh, stopping when I feel her pussy wet and needy.

"So fucking wet for me," I whisper.

"Always," her breath is ragged. "Always have been."

"Bend over the bar and let me see your ass," I command with passion, pushing her down over the edge of the bar.

"People walking by will see us." She looks over her shoulder.

"Good, then there will be no question from anyone about who the hot bartender belongs to."

"So fucking possessive," she chuckles.

"Over you, absolutely." I run the palm of my hand over the globes of her ass, licking my lips as I trace the motion with my gaze. I raise one hand and lower it in a firm smack right over her ass. She instantly winces.

"Luke," she pants.

"You like that?"

"Yes." Her response is direct. I lay one more smack across her skin, turning it the slightest shade of pink in the shape of my hand.

"I fucking told you, pink suits you," I grit out as I unbuckle my pants and drop them to the floor, pooling around my ankles. I pull back and line myself up with her entrance, as she turns and gives me a devilish smile over her shoulder.

"Wanna have a little fun?" she asks.

"What do you have in mind?"

"Well, you told me you wanted me to experience how good it could feel to be promiscuous with the right person." She pauses. "I have a new toy I ordered with some of the indie books from Amazon. One we can use together so you can see how fun toys can be. Maybe then you won't break them like a caveman," she wiggles her brows. "I was going to save it for tonight, but there's no time like the present."

"What kind of toy?" I ask, raising a brow.

"Well, it's really for both of us." She smiles.

"What?" I ask.

She wiggles out of my grip and bends down to her purse on the floor and pulls out a box labeled 'couple's vibrator.' "These two loops," she explains, "go around you, one on your balls, and one around your shaft. This part vibrates on my clit while you fuck me."

"You want to use a fucking toy here on the bar?"

"You just said you wanted everyone to know I belong to you. Now you're getting stage fright?"

Without a word, I pick her up and sit her on the bar, unwrap the toy and slide it over my aching cock. I turn on the vibration and the moan leaving my lips echoes through the mostly empty space. After I climb on top of the bar, I line myself up with her once again. When I slide in, the mix of sensations sends me reeling.

"Shit, this- I, oh my god, Luke," she pants as I slide deep inside her, making sure I don't stop until I feel my head against her cervix. Once there, I pause, making little pulsing motions, and letting the vibration of the toy work over her clit. I watch as her eyes roll back in her head and her breaths become shallow.

I pull her knees up and pin them to my sides with my arms as I continue making small pulsing circles with my cock, buried deep inside her. Watching her like this is the most delicious sight.

"Fuck, baby, you feel incredible." I admire the way she shudders beneath me.

"Luke, I've never felt like this."

"Soak me," I demand. "Soak my cock, baby. Just let go."

I roll one nipple between my teeth. The sensation sends her over the edge.

She thrashes beneath me, her moans and my name echoing off the walls of the dimly lit bar. I watch each quake of her body, as her breaths rise and fall in rapid motion. My balls tighten as her walls clench around me, and with a scream of my name, she does exactly what I was asking–she drenches my balls. The sweet scent of her release fills the room. I pick up my pace, the melody of our skin slapping and the sounds of me pumping in and out of her soaked pussy is a soundtrack I want to play on repeat, as I empty myself inside her.

I collapse on top of her, and we lay there silently until our erratic breaths fall into beat with one another, and I regain enough strength to climb off the bar.

When my feet reach the floor, I step back and take in the vision before me; Blake sweaty, hair a mess, glistening from her own arousal mixed with my own. Her thighs and the counter are both slick, causing me to look down, and admire the mix of our arousal dripping in small beads from the head of my cock, making a tiny puddle on the floor.

"Fuck, B. This is a sight I will never get over."

"Yeah, that was incredible." Her words are faint, and her eyes are hooded.

I'm not sure how long I stood there thinking about her, how breathtaking she is, before we finally cleaned up our mess and made ourselves presentable. But, I'm positive the feeling of me collapsing on top of her, sweat coating our skin and my come sliding out of her, will play on repeat in my head until we make a new memory to take its place.

We cleaned ourselves up, got rid of any evidence of the sex we just had, and ordered pizza to be delivered later. Blake wanted to make sure we had enough to feed everyone coming to help. It's been several hours and we are assembling one of the last three bookshelves as my parents walk in.

"Oh my," mom coos. "This is even better than I imagined," she tells Blake as she wraps her in a tight hug.

"Thanks," Blake responds, a smile covering every inch of her face.

"Where would you like us to start?" Dad asks, giving her a hug.

"I organized all the books by category and placed them in front of the shelves they will go on. There are so many books, I'm not sure there is a logical starting place, so just pick any shelf," Blake directs them towards a few boxes of books.

"Holy shit, this is fucking beautiful," Knox's voice echoes through the small space, just as a tiny figure comes darting through the door, running straight for Blake.

"Blake, Blake, you have books!" Riker yells.

"Sorry, Knox's mom will be here soon to pick him up," Ana calls out, breathless, running through the door after him.

"Hey buddy," Blake smiles, spinning Riker in circles, lathering him in kisses. "I missed you so much."

About an hour goes by before April walks in. When she hits the door, a soft smile crosses her face as she looks around the cozy space. "This is great," she tells Blake as she gives her a soft hug. The tension between them is palpable in the dimly lit room, mirroring the cool air passing outside. I hate how broken their relationship is right now, but appreciate the fact my sister is here for Blake despite their differences.

"Hey Ap," I greet her, placing a kiss on her cheek.

"Hi, brother, this place is amazing." I don't miss the distance in her gaze. I'm used to her giant hugs and bubbly energy, but it is nowhere to be found today.

"Hey, there is a place opening up around the corner offering baking classes. Wanna take one with me next week?" I ask her, knowing how much she loves baking.

"Actually," she lets out a long exhale and I prepare for the let down, but she adds, "a baking class would be fun. I miss our date days."

She spends several hours loading books onto shelves, making conversation with Knox and Ana, but not really directing any of her attention our way. She is obviously avoiding eye contact, as if seeing us together with her own eyes will make our relationship more real.

I can tell it bothers Blake, but baby steps are better than none at all. I know my sister, and how much she loves Blake. This will pass, she just needs time.

When Shit Falls Out of Line

"I could stay awake just to hear you breathing…"
-Aerosmith

Blake

Today has been one of the most amazing yet exhausting days of my life. Luke walked his parents to the car, and I'm standing in the middle of Lit and Libations, taking it all in.

My very own fucking bar.

Luke walks back in and places one hand on the small of my back while he uses his other hand to lay my head on his shoulder. I love that he's content just being there, while I admire my space. I could not have done this without him. Everything has been rapid fire since I took over the space. I can't afford to wait too long to open, so he called in reinforcements to get it all done to ensure I open in two weeks.

The crimson glow of the neon sign behind the bar dances off the crystal tiered chandelier Knox and Ana gifted me. The chandelier scatters red hues into a kaleidoscope of warm shades across the dimly lit room. It feels like the perfect illumination to fill this space, wrapping it in a cozy embrace.

Shelves deliberately placed around the room create cozy reading nooks just begging to be sat in, each one offering something unique, where readers can have a special place to mood read. Pillows and soft cushions accompany each space, with noise canceling headphones they can borrow to tune out the world around them. There are also larger reading spaces that can be reserved for book clubs and outings with friends. Each space is lit by LED candles and supplied with stands for the books they want to discuss, allowing them to be displayed.

As I look around the room, the spines on the bookshelves mix with the red hues cast from the light, creating a tapestry of colors harmonizing the space, enhancing the room's intimate atmosphere. It's a space where the warmth of the light, the scent of books, and the promise of a unique experience intertwine, inviting readers to linger a little longer.

It's turning out better than I imagined.

"I think I like the lights dimmed like this," I tell Luke, "I'm going to go buy some small lamps for the reading nooks, so it always feels this cozy."

"I love that idea." He smiles, kissing me on the head. "Let's go look for them tomorrow, and we can come set them up."

"We will have to go early," I scrunch my nose. "I'm expecting a booze delivery late tomorrow morning, and the rest of the books to arrive early afternoon."

"I'll get you coffee and feed you so you're not a grump all day." He laughs.

About an hour later, after a quick bite to eat and a shower, we cuddle in bed, watching a *Friends* marathon.

"I think I've seen this episode 100 times." He rolls his eyes as Joey slides across the floor on a giant porcelain dog strapped to a cart.

"I love this episode," I giggle. "You really see how much he and Chandler love each other. It reminds me of me and Ana. It was the hardest thing for me when she bought a house and she and Riker moved out. I was so happy for her, but I had a hard time masking how sad I was. This one really resonates."

"I love how much you love them."

I smile. "I really do." I pause for a moment before adding, "But, do you know one good thing that came from not living with them?" I wiggle my brows.

"What's that?"

"That I can have handsome men, all rock hard and full of muscle in my bed every night."

"Men?" I laugh as he tickles my side.

"Well, hard man sounded funny."

"Don't say hard like that, B. I'm so tired, and all I want to do right now is cuddle you, and hold a boob until I fall asleep," he chuckles.

"My boob is not a pacifier," I tease.

"I agree, I'm not putting in my mouth to lull myself to sleep while I suckle," he jokes back. "It's more like a security blanket, if you will."

I gently shove him away, and we cuddle in. Him the big spoon, me the little spoon, and his left arm wrapped tight around my body with his hand, as promised, cupping my right breast. It doesn't take long before I hear his breathing shift over the laughter on the screen, and I snuggle in closer to him, my breath becoming heavy. I pick up the remote lying next to me and turn off the tv, and let the soothing pattern of his breathing lull me into a restful sleep.

Luke

MY ALARM WENT off about 15 minutes ago. It's now 6:15, but Blake didn't stir at the sound of the alarm, so I found myself wanting to lay here for a few more minutes, taking her in. A few minutes turned into 15. We said we'd get up at 6:00 so we could be at the store when it opened at 7:00, but I got a little distracted, and now we're behind schedule.

Blake is curled up in the blankets facing me, her lashes fluttering with every breath, her lips perfectly pursed. She looks so peaceful. Blake loves makeup. Love might actually be an understatement. She doesn't wear much, despite always watching all of those makeup tutorial videos on social media, but for her, like them, it's a creative outlet, an art form. She applies it meticulously, each stroke calculated and magnified by her signature red lipstick. I mean lip stain. She was quick to correct me. Apparently, it's better because it doesn't smudge.

But this Blake, raw and unfiltered, where I can see the texture of her skin, the gentle softness of her features, and the natural flush color of her cheeks, is my favorite version of her. Every detail draws me in–the way her lips curve slightly as she dreams, the delicate rise and fall of her chest with each breath. I can't help but marvel at her beauty, so pure and unguarded at this moment. I want to lie here, and watch her sleep all day long, soaking in the tranquility of her presence. It feels like time stands still, and I can't imagine anything more perfect than her.

I must get lost in my thoughts because I jump, surprised, when I refocus my attention on her face and I see her eyes open, staring back at me.

"Shit, B! I didn't realize you were awake." I shudder.

"I mean, you were staring a hole through my face, lost in whatever you are thinking about," she rebuts.

"I was watching you sleep." I shake my head. "Ok, it sounds creepy. You looked so fucking cute, and I didn't want to wake you, so I just lay here taking you in, and I got lost in my thoughts."

"You're a creeper," she laughs as she climbs out of bed and moves to the clothes she laid out last night.

"Watching me sleep, and now we're late," she huffs. "Looks like a baseball hat and mascara only kind of day."

"Sounds like a fucking win to me. I love when you're dressed down and in a hat. Fuck B, you're always hot."

We spent the morning store-hoping to find the perfect lamp to finish each space. To say I didn't prepare for the amount of detail that would go into picking a damn lamp would be an understatement. I envisioned the process going much faster. I dropped Blake off at L&L when we finally finished and went to pick us up some food. Man, she gets really cranky without food, and because I was "a creeper" this morning, we didn't have time to eat, and we were quickly approaching the Hangry Zone of No Return.

"What do you mean? It won't be here for almost three weeks?" Blake's voice booms across the space as I open the door.

Shit, I should have given her a snack before I left here.

The man standing across from her with an empty dolly just shrugs his shoulders. "Our supplier had a mishap with the shipment and broke a bunch of bottles in transit. There's nothing I can do. Call my boss." He shrugs, handing her a card and walking out the door.

I turn to watch him leave, and then turn back towards Blake. "What was that about?" I ask, setting the bags of food down.

"He unloaded the order, and then handed me the in-voice, and it's short, almost half the order. There is no whisky and no vodka. He said they need about a week to get in the next shipment. It takes about a week to inven-tory it, and then they have to separate it out between all the orders they have to fill before they can deliver. It could take up to three weeks. Luke, we open in two weeks. How the fuck do I open a bar with no whisky and no vodka?" She just stares at me, waiting for an answer.

"Blake, I have no clue, but we will figure something out. It's going to be okay."

"That's always your answer, since we were kids. *We'll figure something out,*" she mocks. "Fuck Luke, can you not be so fucking calm for one second?"

"You're mad at *me* right now?" I ask, looking behind me to make sure her aggression is actually being pointed at me and not some phantom figure behind me. "You're pissed at me because you didn't get an order on time, and can't do anything about it, and I want to help you figure it out?"

"Yes," she says flatly.

"Ok." I keep my eyes on her. "That makes sense."

"Luke, I am freaking out, and you just think it will magically fix itself."

"Nope. Not at all," I argue. "It will 100% not fix itself, you'll have to put on your business owner pants, and come up with a solution, because freaking the fuck out definitely won't fix it."

My heart sounds in my chest, and I cringe inside, waiting for her to erupt. I silently slide the breakfast burrito I picked up across the bar in her direction and wait.

She stares at it for a second, and then leisurely unwraps it, taking small bites at first, but they quickly turn into giant bites, and before I know it, the entire thing is gone. She takes a sip of the diet coke I also brought her, and then takes in a long inhale. "Ok. Let's think."

That's it? What the fuck.

Hesitant, I suggest going to get bottles from a local liquor store. She considers it for a second before responding.

"I can't. I have to purchase all the alcohol from a licensed wholesaler."

So, here we are creating an opening night menu she can carry into the first week if needed without the two missing alcohols.

"Ok, so we have a mojito, an adonis, an amaretto sour, Aperol Spritz and sour, a gin martini, mint julep, and various wines and beer options." She sighs in relief. "Now, I just have to tweak the recipes to put my spin on them and come up with a name for all of them to put on the menu."

I walk over and give her a light kiss. "Do you feel good about the menu?" I ask.

"As good as I can. I feel like I have a good variety, so it shouldn't even be noticeable. Thank you," she melts into our kiss.

I look down at my watch and realize it is now 5:15. "We better get you some food again before you have another hangry spell." I laugh.

"I was not hangry," she protests.

"No? You only inhaled your burrito like you were carb loading for the Olympics for fun, and then magically became level headed again?" I tease.

She bumps my shoulder with hers, ignoring my comment, "Let's go get burgers. I might need another carb load for our little marathon later." She winks.

"Oh, you think so?" I ask.

"Yes," she grabs her purse and walks out the door.

Perfection is Fleeting

"Oh, kiss me beneath the milky twilight"
-Sixpence None The Richer

Blake

"STILL NOT IDEAL, BUT I appreciate the update," I tell the vendor on the phone. She just called to update me on the shipment I am waiting for. I know it is not their fault, so I try really hard to control my emotions when speaking to her. Her company is also in a tight spot, and she is throwing in a few promotional items for free with my order for the inconvenience.

"What are you up to beautiful?" Luke whispers in a velvety tone as he comes up behind me, rubbing my shoulders.

"Just got off the phone with the vendor. She said they're going to deliver my order a few days early and are throwing in a few free promotional items for the inconvenience." I turn to him with a crooked smile.

"You know what?" he asks with a raised brow. "I have a few days off, and you're all caught up for the opening. Let's take a little retreat for the night."

"A retreat to where?" I ask.

"It's a surprise." His grin is delicious. "You go to the bar and tie up any loose ends so you can relax, and I'll handle everything else."

"What should I pack?"

"Nothing. I've got it all handled." He smiles.

"Fuck no! If we are going somewhere, I want to make sure I am prepared and have the right clothes," I argue.

"Well, the only one who will see you is me, so as long as I like them, that's all that matters. To be honest, you won't really need them, anyway." He slaps me on the ass and ushers me out the door.

Butterflies swirl in my stomach and my mind buzzes with curiosity as I make my way to the bar. There is something about surprises that just makes me so happy, and the thought of being at Luke's mercy for the night makes the thought even better.

I stop at the lingerie store around the corner to pick him out a little surprise of his own on my way.

I make my way to the back of the small store to the display of intimate sets. I am not a fan of lingerie. My thighs are a little thick and my boobs are a little small, not really being blessed with curves in places show-cased by lingerie, so it always feels a little lackluster to me when I put it on.

I'm fumbling through the racks, making my second lap around a small selection, when I hear a soft voice over the sound of the soft music filling the space, offering a soothing melody crooning through the speakers.

The shop is small, with only about 10 racks and a few shelves scattered through the space. Each section labeled with a small sign hanging overhead. There are sections for basics and essentials, shapewear, and intimates.

I peek over the rack and catch sight of a short, elderly woman standing just on the other side. Her hair, a soft cloud of white, styled in tight, neat curls, framing her face with a touch of elegance. She's dressed in a soft pink blouse, paired with black slacks, hanging effortlessly at her sides. Her black orthopedic shoes are practical and sturdy, yet still enhance the elegance of her look.

A beautiful string of yellow pearls drapes around her neck, with matching earrings dangling from her ears. She embodies the picture-perfect image of a grandmother-warm, approachable, and timeless.

My gaze shifts to her face where her makeup is far more pronounced than most women her age.

A soul that mirrors mine.

The soft blush on her cheeks, the bold outline of her eyes, and the vibrant lipstick are a deliberate contrast to the natural gentleness of her features and clothes, begging to stand out. It's as though she's crafted a persona, not just for today, but for a lifetime, and it's both striking and unexpected.

"Sorry, what was that?" I ask, realizing I was so struck by her beautiful appearance, I didn't catch what she said.

"If you'd like, I can help you find the perfect piece," she offers with a warm smile.

"Oh, it's ok. I'm sure you need to find what you are looking for," I respond, returning the warm smile.

She puts her hand out and shakes mine. "I'm Lily. Welcome to Lily's Lace Parlour."

I cough. "You own this shop? It's beautiful."

"You seem surprised, dear."

"No, I um… Well, a little," I respond shyly, slightly ashamed of my surprise.

"Oh dear, trust me, you're not the only one. Most people get uncomfortable with someone resembling their grandmother helping them pick intimates, but trust me, I have the experience you need to select just the right set," she suggests with a wink. "So, what are you looking for?"

Taken aback by her candid demeanor and bright smile, I tap into her expertise. "Well, my boyfriend is taking me away for the night to a surprise location. I wanted to get him something special in return."

"Oh, my favorite occasion-spontaneity. Tell me a bit about him, about the two of you," she insists.

"Well, we have known each other for many years, but just started dating. He's my best friend's older brother. He's quite a bit older than me, so I want something sure to catch his attention. I'm sure he's seen quite a few pieces of lingerie before."

"How much older? What's his age?" she asks with a quizzical look.

"He's 38," I answer.

"Oh, late 30s are my favorite age. They are sophisticated, charming, and have enough experience to to take exactly what they want. But, not to the age where help is necessary." She punctuates her words with a playful wink. "What do you like and dislike the most about intimate wear, dear?"

I ponder on this for a second before I respond, "It's beautiful, and in most cases, lace and rich colors can enhance features perfectly. You know, making men go crazy, but I have a hard time finding pieces to flatter my build. All my curves are outside of the lingerie zone, so I never feel sexy."

"I know just the set," she announces with a little pep in her step and a small chuckle.

"This," she hands me an emerald green set. "The balconette style top creates just enough lift and volume without overwhelming the chest. Oh, and these high-waisted, cheeky bottoms help create the illusion of length between the hips and thighs, plus they show off a little tush, and by the looks of it, you have a good one." She winks.

I take the delicate set in my hands and walk into the dressing room.

After adjusting the straps, I turn around in awe of the sight in the mirror. The dark shade of emerald enhances the ember hues of my hair as they cascade over the delicate lace patterns lightly covering the peak of my nipples, with them slightly peeking through the thin veil of the fabric. The high waist cut of the bottoms does just as Lily promised, accentuating the length of my legs, creating a space between them and my hips, showing a sensual curve of the globes of my ass. I have never felt sexier.

More than happy with what she pulled for me, I get dressed and meet Lily at the register, promising another return.

"You made me fall in love with lingerie, and with myself in it," I say to Lily as she places my purchase in a dainty pink box adorned with a black lace ribbon.

She scurries around the corner and gives me a tight grandmother, like hug when I hear the bells over the door ding.

I finish talking to Lily and turn to see April at the back of the store, looking at the intimate sets where I just was. A knot forms in my stomach and instead of rushing over to her like I usually would, I quickly turn and scurry out the door before she spots me. I'm not sure seeing me buy lingerie for her brother is something she'd appreciate at the moment.

But as I step into the cool night air, that knot doesn't loosen, it only tightens, like I'm running from something I should be ready to face.

Luke

BLAKE HAS BEEN QUIET for the entire drive. I'm guessing she has a lot on her mind with the opening of the bar quickly approaching. Talking isn't high on my list right now, either. I went to lunch with my sister today, like we often do. I tried to broach the conversation of Blake and I. It was not great, she is so reluctant to let the idea of us in, even though I have told her time and time again, she would never lose either of us.

I can't wait to get Blake away for the night, to be alone with her, under the stars, back to where we first let ourselves entertain the idea of us.

As if she is just now breaking the fog of her inner dialogue, she looks around and marvels at the view surrounding us. The rolling hill and plush landscape, a tapestry of various shades of green and yellow. The end of summer, just before fall, in Vermont is my favorite. Especially with Blake by my side, usually wearing little clothing because of the warm temperatures.

"This road looks familiar. Have I been up here before?" Just as she asks, we pass a thick wall of trees to the clearing we occupied not too long ago.

"Luke, is this where we came camping?" She puts her hands in the air in excitement.

"Nevermind, it is. I burned the landscape over there into my memory when I avoided eye contact with you after you saw me fucking a vibrator in my tent." She laughs, pointing straight ahead at another line of trees.

"Precisely why I wanted to come back here. I have great luck here." I laugh.

Blake and I spend the next hour setting up our tent, settling all our belongings, and getting the food out of the coolers. It all goes much quicker than last time because tonight we will be sharing a tent. Knowing neither of us would want to cook, I went to the market and made a charcuterie board with a variety of meats, cheeses, crackers, fruits, and relishes. I also grabbed a bottle of apple whisky, some ginger ale and limes, the ingredients for Blake's favorite drink. I start a fire while Blake mixes us up some drinks, and we settle in on an oversized camping chair for two I splurged on for this very occasion.

"Adult lunchable, whisky and a camping couch, damn I should have been going after old guys all along. Age really *does* make you wiser," she laughs, handing me my drink.

"You're such a brat sometimes," I tease, taking my drink and pulling her onto my lap.

"Oh, you have no idea just how bratty I can be." She nips my earlobe with a playful bite.

I hiss and pull her in closer. "Maybe I should remind you what happens when you act this way."

"Please, remind me. I wouldn't want to make you mad," she says in a sardonic tone.

Without warning, I pick her up, and turn her so she is facing the new camping chair and wrap my hand around her throat from behind. "Spread your legs and put your hands on the back of the chair."

Without question, she does as I say. She leans far over the seat of the chair so her hands sit on the backrest, the position extenuating the curves of her ass in her tight shorts. I had an outfit picked out for her when she got home, my favorite jean shorts, a tank top which shows the perfect amount of cleavage, and a hat. I let her pick the shoes.

I run my hands up her inner right thigh, and then back down the left with my face close enough to smell her arousal. Her breath hitches when my lips press to her skin, little red marks left behind from my beard. Beard rash between her legs is my fucking favorite. I kiss her legs as my arms snake around her body and unbutton her shorts. Methodically, I pull them down and immediately notice a pair of emerald panties, ones I am sure I have never seen before. "What's this?" I ask, snapping the lacy fabric against her porcelain skin.

She deliberately turns, throwing her hat on the chair and peeling the tank top off over her head. My mouth goes dry when I see a matching bra perfectly cupping each breast, showing her perfect nipples below the lace fabric. I look down at her body, and Blake is pure perfection, like always, but this lingerie set, fuck me, it frames her features perfectly, as if made only for her. The glow of the fire cascades across her skin, accentuating each curve, the emerald green a beautiful contrast to her red hair as it hangs in waves.

"Baby, this is, Fuck!" I kiss every inch of her body, not knowing where to start. "Spread your legs and bend back over so I can appreciate your body in this fucking thing," I continue, running my hand over my erection in my pants.

"So bossy," she teases.

"You have no idea just how bossy I can be."

I continue to kiss her body until I reach the bottom of her ass where her cheeks meet her legs. When I find myself in the perfect viewpoint, I slide her panties to the side, exposing her lips dripping for me, and the puckered hole of her perfect ass. Gently, I run my thumb over the opening and she flinches but doesn't protest, so I circle it one more time. "One day, this ass will be mine," I promise as I work my way down to her soaked pussy. "But right now, this needs my attention."

I slide one finger inside and then add another. The sounds of her arousal mix with the crackle of the fire, creating the most amazing symphony. "Oh, baby, you are so fucking wet."

"Fuck me Luke. I can't do foreplay right now. Please, just fuck me," she begs.

"No. You surprised me with this. I want to enjoy it. Get on your knees," I demand.

Again, she submits without question. While she makes her way to the ground and gets on her knees, on a blanket I strategically placed before we sat down, I unbuckle my pants and pull them down, my cock springing free. I nudge her lips with the head of my cock, and she opens, sucking me all the way inside. A loud groan immediately leaves my mouth.

She sucks me in and out, simultaneously working my dick with her delicate hands, applying the perfect amount of pressure with each pass. After a few minutes, my attention shifts to one of her hands as it slithers down her body towards her clit. I let her circle it once, just enough to give a little pressure, before I speak. "Enough, B. You will not come on your hand, you will come on my dick. Do you hear me?"

She pulls away. "Luke, I need to come."

"Then you better suck a little faster, baby, because this conversation is making me lose focus, and the sight of your lips stretched around my dick with fucking lingerie on is making my fucking night."

She sucks again, picking up the same momentum as before. "Such a good fucking girl, B. So fucking obedient," I praise, running my hand through her hair.

The sound of her mouth around my cock, the sight of her like this, and the idea of her warm, wet pussy are creating a familiar tug in my balls. Knowing I'm going to come, I abruptly pull out of her mouth, pull her up and turn her around, pushing her shoulders forward so she is bent over the chair. I crash inside her, pumping in and out at a ferocious pace until she is screaming my name. Her words echo in the silence surrounding us, alone in the woods. I feel her pussy clench around me and the sensation creates the same profound fervor within my balls. Before I know it, we are both coming with loud pants and bated breath.

Blake and I took a few minutes to get our wits about us as we came down from our post sex high, but now we are by the fire cuddled under the blanket, enjoying our apple whisky and ginger ales... well, our second, or maybe third.

"Nope, I think this is our fourth," Blake responds, causing me to realize I was questioning our number of drinks out loud.

"You seem drunk," I slur.

"You do too. You can't even remember how many drinks we've had." She giggles as she swirls the contents of her glass.

I lean over and brush the hair from her shoulder so I can kiss her neck and see the strap of her bra peeking out.

"Where did you get this? We need it in every color," I ask, playing with the strap.

"There is a cute little boutique around the corner from the bar. It's called Lily's Lace Parlour," she tells me. "I actually saw April there."

"Yeah, what was she up to?" I ask.

"I don't know. I dodged her and left before she saw me."

I don't respond. I'm not sure what to say.

She fills the silence with a sudden rant. "I didn't know what to do. I wasn't sure how she would respond. She would have known I bought this for you, and she is already so feking pis- so ferking mad," she slurs.

"She will get over it, B. She just needs time," I reassure her, taking the drink out of her hand and standing, taking her hand. "Let's get some sleep. We've both had too much to drink."

I usher her to the tent and get her settled in bed. Then I make my way back out to the fire, pick up all of our food and trash, and put out the fire. When I get back to the tent, Blake is fast asleep, her face aglow from the light on her phone screen.

She must have fallen asleep scrolling. So fucking cute.

I pick up her phone and notice her message app is open to a text she just sent to April.

> **Blake:** Don't worry. I can handle Luke. I know you think we're not ready, but I think we are perfect.

> **April:** Well, I'm glad you can handle him, whatever that means.

I stare at the text and cringe.

Fuck.

Shame—Fuck Her

"Why can't we be friends…"
-Smash Mouth

Blake

"Fuck, fuck, fuck," I whisper to myself as I scurry around the tent throwing clothes on. I am trying my hardest to be quiet so I don't wake Luke, but fail.

"What, what happened?" He shoots up and starts running around mimicking my motions, gathering the clothes he wore last night now scattered on the floor next to our blowup mattress.

I chuckle. "I love how you're matching my energy right now. Blindly, I might add, but it's fine. Well, it's not fine." A ragged breath escapes me. "I sent a drunk text to April last night, leaving a little too much open for interpretation, and it pissed her off. She's probably more pissed now because I passed out and didn't see it until this morning. I have to smooth things over."

"I saw it come through. I texted her and told her you had been drinking, but she didn't respond." He laces his arms around me, attempting to comfort me, but this isn't something Luke and I can work out.

"Were you going to just leave me here?" he asks.

"Obviously not," I chuckle nervously. "I was going to pick things up."

"You are such a little liar. You were totally going to leave me here in your panic," he jokes, catching on to my little secret shameful admission.

Guess my face gives me away.

"I guess I'll forgive you this time. I know it's hard to think clearly with a hangover, especially when you're emotional."

"I am not hungover or emotional," I protest.

"Really? The smell of whisky oozing out of your pores tells a different story, and need I remind you I woke up to you in a panic, ready to leave my ass here with no car and no goodbye?"

"Can you please just help me pack up so I can go talk to her?" I began unzipping the tent and stepping out to a dimly lit sky and the chill of the morning air.

"Blake, it's only 5:12 am," I hear Luke groan as I zip the tent closed and continue to panic pack and throw things in the car. "She and I are going to a baking class tomorrow. I can talk to her then."

"Tomorrow? Are you crazy? That's an entire day away."

Luke and I got everything packed up pretty quickly and when we got home, he told me to head over to April's and he'd unpack his car and put everything away.

That was about an hour ago. I stopped at the coffee shop around the corner from April's getting a peace offering and have now been standing at her door for about 15 minutes, trying to build up the courage to knock.

Taking one last soothing breath, I lift my hand and knock it softly on the door.

A few seconds later, the door opens and April is standing on the other side, staring at me without a word.

"I brought coffee," I offer, holding up her cup. The smell of cinnamon rolls fills the doorway. April runs her own bakery a few blocks from here, but it's closed on Sunday mornings. She rarely bakes at home, but I can tell by the look on her face these are rage baking cinnamon rolls right now. Baking calms her down.

Fuck.

She still doesn't respond. She just moves to the side and gestures for me to come inside.

"April, I-" She puts her hand up.

"I need food and coffee before I can have this conversation," she states. Taking two cinnamon rolls off the tray and handing one to me. "You smell like a brewery. How much did you drink?"

"A lot," I respond, taking a bite.

She says nothing in return, and neither do I. We just sit here in silence until our cinnamon rolls are gone and we have both drank the coffee filling our cups.

When I build up the courage, I start. "April, I reread my text this morning. I'm sorry. I know what I said came out wrong."

"Yeah. It did."

"I didn't mean to upset you. I was drunk and upset. Yesterday, I was at Lily's and I left before you saw me. Last night, I got drunk and unloaded on Luke about seeing you. It made me nervous to see you, so I just left. I thought you'd be mad I was getting something, knowing it was for Luke-" She cuts me off for the second time.

"This," she slaps her hand on the counter. "This is the problem, B. This is exactly what I was worried about. You are not in a place to be the woman he needs you to be. He is coming off of a divorce and needs stability-"

Now I cut her off. "This is the second fucking time you have said that to me. What the fuck do you mean by that?"

"If you would let me finish, I would tell you." She takes a breath. "He needs someone who is emotionally in a good place, who is void of drama and confusion. You need that too, but neither one of you is there. If you were, you would have never dodged me. You would have come up to me like an adult and said hi to your best friend.

Regardless of what you thought I'd think. You'd prove to me you were in a loving, comfortable relationship."

"I didn't want to make you uncomfortable."

"That, B, does make me uncomfortable. You're so unsure of your relationship you can't face me head on. When you saw me in public, you avoided me. You hide your relationship from me when we are together, even though I know it's happening. You never talk to me about it. The day we set up the bar, you acted like you didn't even know him. You refuse to let me see you two together, so I can see how happy you are, and how real it is. You shield me, so what I've been afraid of is already happening. I've lost you. I'm not your best friend. You treat me as if I'm just Luke's sister." She takes a long breath and I don't know what to say to fill the uncomfortable void between us.

She takes a few sips of her coffee and continues to avoid making eye contact with me. "You are both still figuring things out and I worry at the first sign of tension in your relationship you won't make it, and I will lose you. He's my brother, B. I have to pick him."

"So you're already counting your losses before we've even really started?" I ask with hurt and insecurity lacing my words, a feeling I am becoming all too familiar with and I hate it. "You think I'm not enough for him? We're just doomed from the start?"

"*That* is not what I said," she responds quickly.

"No, but it's what you meant." I stand and grab my things and walk out the door. She is right, and leaving is easier than facing the truth. She doesn't follow me, she doesn't even try to stop me.

And I don't blame her.

Luke

I GOT ALL THE food and camping stuff unpacked and put away. I decided Blake could probably use a relaxing day when she gets back, so I ordered pizza and rented a movie. She texted me about 20 minutes ago saying she was on her way home. Just as I reach for my phone to see the time, she opens the front door. Tears are streaming down her face in a silent cry, her eyes red and swollen. Small red splotches cover her face and neck, and she looks painstakingly defeated.

Fucking hell.

"Baby, what happened?" I ask, walking over to her and wrapping her in a hug.

"She said I treat her like your sister instead of my best friend, and she has already lost me." Her words break into a soft sob. "And she's right, I do. I don't think she believes we will make it, or that I'm worthy of your love."

"She said that?" I prod, disbelieving April actually feels that way about Blake. She adores her.

"No, but she insinuated it."

"Maybe you misunderstood what she was saying. She loves you. She thinks the world of you. I think she is afraid that if things don't work out, she will lose you," I try to reassure her, but she pulls away.

"You think we won't work? What, are you just waiting for the smallest thing to happen so you can leave?"

I'm stunned by her sudden change in demeanor. This shattered, unsure version of the strong woman I have loved all these years. "B, look at me. I've been waiting to be with you for five years. When I asked you to move in with me, I meant it, and I never want you to leave. I'm fucking more than sure about us," I affirm, putting both hands around her face and pulling her into me until my forehead is on hers. "I just think it is something she worries about because she loves you, sh–"

My work phone buzzes on the counter. I close my eyes, raking my hands over my face, ignoring it for a second. When it buzzes two more times, I have to check it. I place a kiss on her forehead and walk over to my phone.

"Fuck. There was a big accident. They need extra people. I have to go. Get some rest, please. I ordered pizza and rented a movie. I'll be back as soon as I can, OK?" I can't believe I have to leave her right now.

"I'm actually exhausted. I'm sorry I unloaded on you, and got all dramatic." A shy smile crosses her lips.

"You can always fall apart with me, B. I'm not going anywhere." I kiss her forehead and walk out the door.

I've been at the hospital for about two hours now and it's been nothing but chaos since the first ambulance got here. A fucking drunk driver crashed into the side of a car with two college boys coming home from a soccer tournament. Their car spun around and hit the one behind it, filled with one of the boy's family. There were 7 people in total between the two cars. 5 teens and two adults. The 3 kids in the car with the adults were in high school. Their oldest son is home from college driving behind the family with his buddy in the car. I got the entire run down from the dad while I was treating him. I think talking was keeping him calm. Most of them had minor injuries, but the oldest son, the driver of the car struck by the drunk driver, still hasn't come in. Apparently, he's pinned between the steering wheel and seat, and they were working to cut him out when they made the rest of the family and his passenger leave to get treated. The poor mom is freaking out. We had to give her medication to calm her down.

The drunk driver was banged up pretty badly, but after running a code, we were able to stabilize him enough for surgery, and now I'm stitching up the dad's hand while we wait for word on his son. He's a talker, just like I am in stressful situations. It's interesting, talking to a reflection of yourself.

"Our son, Adam, is the one driving the other car. He plays on his college soccer team," his voice is shaky. "He is such a hard worker. I should have listened to my wife and driven his car. It would be me pinned in there, not my boy."

"He sounds like a great kid," I reassure him. "You know what? I have to go check on another patient, but I'll send Cash Easton in. He's volunteering here, and loves talking sports. Talking to him might be a good distraction while you wait," I offer as I leave the room.

I'm not a fan of Cash right now, given the recent information I learned about him and Blake, but he is great with people, and I know he will keep the dad calm.

I turn and make my way to the doors, closing the curtain behind me. The ambulance with Adam just pulled up. The EMTs bring the gurney in and when they park it, all the air leaves my lungs. Adam looks just like my friend DJ from high school. Spitting fucking image of my best friend. They are carbon copies of each other. Blond curly hair, light freckles across the nose, tall, muscular, one of those people who had natural muscle tone. Lightly tanned skin, and a pointed nose.

A drunk driver killed DJ the summer between our junior and senior year. I was with him. The memories of him in the driver's seat next to me, limp and unresponsive, still haunt my dreams many nights. I had years of thera-py to overcome the pain and guilt I felt over his death.

He had picked me up for a party, but we never made it there. So the sight in front of me is haunting. I feel the air in my lungs become sparse, and sweat breaks out on my forehead and neck.

Suddenly, I'm right back to being 17, sitting across from my parents in the hospital waiting room as they try to tell me DJ didn't make it.

I remember the accident in vivid detail, burned in my memory like a scar branded from a hot poker, a dagger penetrating my soul.

They said he died on impact. He didn't suffer, but I had a hard time believing them. I was there, in the car, next to him, and the sight before me didn't match their words.

When I looked at him, he didn't look gone at all. He was sitting in the awkward position you find yourself in when you fall asleep in the car, head leaning against the seatbelt. He looked like he was just sleeping. His hands were still gripping the wheel, like he was still holding on, stunned by the impact. There was no blood, he didn't have any visible bruising from what I could see. In my memories, I looked worse off than him. There were no physical signs of injury. The other car hit my side. I took the brunt of the impact, but somehow he is gone and I'm still here.

I still have a hard time digesting their words and what I saw, even after all the medical training I've had. My 17-year-old brain immediately takes over, and nothing makes sense.

The doctors had said he broke his neck, the impact of the collision shook him around just enough for a fatal injury. They said the direction of the impact jolted him in such a way that his head hit the side of the door before banging it back in the other direction at such a fast pace and it severed his spinal cord, but I don't remember any of it. We were driving, then we were spinning, and then we stopped, and before I knew it there were sirens and we were both being rushed to the hospital.

Snapping back to the present, I take a breath and then I move in fast steady motions, acting quickly to tend to all of Adam's wounds, hook him up to fluid and oxygen. While my body is moving quickly in precisely calculated motions I have trained for, my heart is in shreds, and my brain is moving in slow motion, memorizing every feature of what I picture as my childhood best friend laying on the table in front of me, memories of that night flooding my brain.

We are working frantically to prepare him for surgery, as he has a collapsed lung and a few minor broken bones. His condition is critical, but stable, and the prognosis has mixed emotions rising in me. Hope and loss swirl around inside me, colliding like the bumper cars I used to ride as a kid. I'm having a hard time reconciling the two emotions, as I fight to turn them off and do what I have been trained to do. I cling to the clinical guidelines, fighting the rising tide of helplessness, striving for objectivity against the overwhelming emotional current. There is no room for emotions when treating life-threatening injuries, but today, right now, that is something I am finding it hard to do.

We Were So Close

"Do you have to, do you have to, do you have to let it linger?"
-The Cranberries

Blake

LUKE WAS GONE ALL night. I had a hard time sleeping, so I watched old reruns of Reba until I fell asleep. Last time I looked at the clock, it was 3:18am. Now, it's 7:37am. I'm in the kitchen brewing coffee and making a bowl of cereal. The embarrassment I felt over my reaction was too much to handle. Between the emotions, the alcohol, and the fear of being deserted by the only authentic version of family I have ever known, I lost it.

My mom was not a mom, not in the traditional sense. She made sure I had food, clothes, and a place to lay my head after a long day, but she wasn't a mom. I was secondary to whichever man occupied her bed, so the Jennings became my found family.

To hear April say, *"He's my brother, B. I have to pick him,"* stung with such a piercing force, I felt my DNA shift at that moment. Realization struck, as much as I see them as my family, that's a coveted sentiment I have not truly earned the right to claim.

Our relationship is conditional, and this is something I am not sure I will ever truly unpack.

I hoped April would call, maybe if she'd text it would make her words sting less, but then again, why would she? Every turn I make is a misstep. I need to call her, be her friend again, not her brother's girlfriend, but in my fragile state, I'm having a hard time finding the courage.

I have never felt so distant from her, even in the years we didn't see each other. I hear a shuffling noise behind me, followed by something hitting the floor, and turn to see Luke standing next to his dropped bag.

"Morning, babe, you look exhausted." I smile, walking over to him. The closer I get, the more noticeable the red rim around his eyes are. He looks up at me, tears in his eyes. Panic surges through me. "What happened?"

He doesn't say a word, he just slides down the wall in silent sobs. Unsure what the fuck to do, I grab his phone from the floor next to him and start frantically looking through his texts and call log for any hint of what the fuck may have happened. When I come up empty-handed, I set the phone down and gently place his face between my hands and straddle him.

"Luke, what happened? Please, baby, please, please," I chant.

After a few long breaths, he stutters, "The k-k-kid in the accident. It was my friend, DJ."

He breaks into another sob as I try to put the pieces together in my mind. I remember hearing about his friend DJ when April and I were in high school. His mom was always worried when we went out. She never allowed us to drive ourselves to parties. One of April's parents always took us and picked us up. DJ died in an accident on the way to a party when Luke was in high school. Even 12 years later, when April and I were in highschool, the loss still haunted his family. It was a long time ago, so I'm having a hard time putting the pieces together now. What is Luke talking about? What happened tonight that brought him back there?

"Luke, baby, what do you mean?" I wrap my arms around him and pull him into a hug.

A breath later, he responds. "The kid in the accident I was called to, he was with his friend, they got hit by a drunk driver, and fuck B, he looked exactly like DJ."

My stomach churns and my heart clinches at his words. He was with DJ that night, in the car. This has to be tearing him apart. Resurfacing old wounds.

After several hours of Luke sitting in silence on the couch staring at the black screen of the tv he never turned on, I called his mom. Maggie will know what to do. She always does.

I have tried to comfort him in every way I know how. He cried while I held him, head in my lap, as we lay on the couch. I made him some hot tea and a snack. I even tried to talk to him about it, but he was unresponsive.

His mom came with his dad in tow a few minutes ago, and for reasons I don't understand, now, with them, he's got nothing but chatter on the brain. He told them everything, unloaded his feelings and thoughts in rapid fire.

I know it's not fair of me to be upset right now. I know he's grieving old wounds. Maybe it's because my mom and I aren't close, and I learned at a young age I couldn't count on her, that I'm having a hard time understanding. I'm his girlfriend, I've known him for years, we love each other. I would have thought he would have needed me in this situation, at least to hold his hand, but it seems like all he really needed was his mom. That feeling is so foreign to me, but in all reality, if I needed a mom, I'd call Maggie too.

Trying to push my own feelings aside, I go to the kitchen and make us all something to eat.

"Lucas, you need to call and schedule an appointment with Ginger. Immediately," I hear his dad state in a no bullshit tone. "This was hard on you the first time, and could easily spiral if you let it."

"I know. I just, I have to make sure he's ok. The kid. He has to be ok." Luke stands from the couch and grabs his keys off the coffee table.

"I made you all something to eat." I set the sandwiches and chips on the coffee table.

"I can't eat, you guys enjoy. I'm going to go check on Adam." He sighs, walking out the door, not listening to any of our pleas for him to stay.

I stare at the lean curves of his back, noting the tension in his muscles as he closes the door behind him. I wish there was something I could do to make it better.

Luke

I WALK INTO THE hospital deciding Blake was right, I need to eat something or I'm going to be sick.

Shit, she made me lunch, and I just ignored it and walked out.

When I get home, I'll apologize. I know it seems ridiculous, but seeing this kid who looks like DJ was a punch in the gut. This wasn't a reaction I ever expected at work. I've worked on so many hit and runs, accidents involving teens, many of them also involving drunk drivers and have never felt this way. Maybe it's being back home, maybe it's the circumstances of this accident, but above all else, I think it's his face.

I stop at a cart in the lobby and grab a protein bar, and shovel it down on the elevator ride up. Deciding I can't see his face again, I opt to talk with Adam's nurses instead. I make my way over to the nurses' station to find a tall brunette coming out of his room. I can see his mom, tired and defeated, in the door's crack as the nurse closes it behind her.

Pulling out my ID, I greet her, "Hey, I'm Dr. Jennings. I work in the ER and treated him when he came in. I wanted to follow up on his injuries and see how he's doing."

She hands me the iPad in her hand containing his chart as she speaks. "He's in terrible shape. He has a few broken ribs, causing his lung to collapse. And he has several broken bones, but the biggest concern right now is his kidney function. His creatinine is extremely low, and he has very little urine output. Doctors are meeting in a few minutes to come up with a plan."

"Damn it, how is everyone else doing?" I ask.

"Shaken up, mom's a mess. So talk to them. They would probably love to know you came up to check on him."

"Sorry, I actually have another patient I need to check on," I lie in response, knowing I would fall apart if I talked to her. "I have to get going. Can you let them know I came by?" I turn and walk down the hallway, an undeniable pang in my chest.

When I reach the elevator and the doors open, it takes all of my strength to step inside, instantly leaning on the wall behind me. Staring at my feet, I reason with myself. It would have been impossible for me to save DJ. I didn't know how. I did all I could to prepare Adam while he was in the ER so he can make a strong and successful recovery. Rational thoughts have to be my anchor.

The door dings and opens to the main lobby of the hospital. There is only one thing I need right now, a drink.

I walk to the bar where Blake used to work to get a quick drink, but when I walk in, there are a few guys from work playing darts and having drinks. They call me over the second they spot me.

"Luke," I hear Jay yell across the bar, standing from the table by the dartboard.

"Hey," I sit down next to him.

"You look like a pile of shit," he laughs. "Be back in a sec." He scurries away to talk to a brunette he was clearly eyeing around me.

"Did you just get off?" A voice behind me says. I turn and see Ty.

"No, I worked late last night, just stopped by to check on one of my patients."

"Yeah, I came in this morning. They said it was pretty bad last night." He says, just standing there.

"It's early. I'm surprised you're already off. Do you want to sit down?"

"No, I'm good. I just had some paperwork to do today. I wasn't technically working." He looks around the bar uncomfortably, "I'm meeting-"

"Hey stranger," Isa nudges my hand as she slides into the chair across from me.

"Isa," Ty continues with a suspicious smile.

"You said no one else wanted to meet up tonight," she looks right at Ty.

"Luke never responded to my text, and Keith said he was out," he says, making a weird ass face at me.

"Well then, I'll go get us a round," Isa offers, standing from her seat, and Ty gets up quickly to join her at the bar. As I watch them walk away, I look at my texts to confirm I'm not crazy. Ty never texted me.

Hmmm.

"Beers all around, but I got you a whisky as well. You look like you could use something a little stronger." Ty hands me two glasses.

"Yeah, the last 24 hours have been a motherfucker." I opt for the amber liquid first.

I close my eyes, taking the shot and letting the warm burn from the whisky fill my body as it traces the path down my throat to my stomach, offering a sense of relief I have been chasing all day. There is just something about the burn from whisky that is therapeutic to me, a relief nothing else can offer. Without hesitation, I grab the glass of beer and chug it too, disappointed by the cool crisp sensation as it extinguishes the burn. The relief is not the same, so when I go to the bar to order the next round, I make mine a double.

"Luke, you should probably drink some water," Ty proposes, handing me a glass.

"It's just, it makes the burn away," I respond, knowing the words tangle in my throat.

"Isa, grab his phone and call Blake. He can't drive," Ty gently instructs, refilling the glass of water I just chugged.

"Hey doll," I can barely hear what Isa is saying with her back turned to me. "We're with Luke at the bar and he can't drive. He really needs to get out of here." There is a long pause, followed by a few nods and mumbles. "Yep… ok. Sounds good. See you in a few."

She hands me my phone and orders some fries. "I think you could use some food," she firmly recommends.

When the fries come, I inhale them, feeling like I haven't eaten in days. I barely take a breath between bites. I look up to grab my water and see a flash of red hair come through the door.

B, my girl. There she is.

It feels like it only took her a few seconds to get here.

Was she sitting in the car outside?

I give her a soft smile as I shove the last few fries into my mouth.

"Hey, B."

"Hey," she nods. She smiles, but I don't think it reaches her eyes. I can't really tell because her eyes are fuzzy, and she looks a little sad.

"Shit, baby. I want your sandwich. I was just not thinkering, Isa ordered the fries." My words are a rambling mess.

"Not sure what that means," Isa laughs, confusion in her eyes. "He needed food, so we ordered him some fries. Is he not supposed to eat fries?"

"Not sure either," Blake arches a brow. "Thanks for feeding him. I'm not sure he's eaten all day."

Ty wraps his arm around my shoulder and lifts me off the chair.

"We'll follow you guys home and help you get him in the house. I think he's gotten worse since we called you." He slides his other hand in his pocket and hands his wallet to Isa. "Can you pay the tab?"

"Yeah, I'll meet you outside," she offers him a playful smile.

"Are you two hooking up?" I whisper in his ear. Well, I thought I was whispering, but based on his reaction, it might have been a bit louder than I intended.

"What?" he hisses. "No, thanks to you. She will probably just go home after we drop you off."

"Oh, so you want to, then?" I laugh. "It should been clear when," a hiccup interrupts my words, "when you lie about texting me," I slur with a wobble.

We are walking to the car. Blake parked right outside the door. Why is it taking so long to get to it?

Blake hits the unlock button and Ty slides me inside.

A few minutes later, we leave the parking lot, headed home. Blake doesn't say much on the way home outside of asking me if I'm ok. She rolled down the window and told me to cool my face in case I puke.

"B, are you mad at me?" I ask.

"Luke, I'm not mad at you. You just need to sleep it off," she coaxes as Ty opens the door again. I turn to look at him and everything becomes fuzzy, black infiltrating the lights in the parking garage as we make our way towards the elevator.

Dreams... Come... True...

"Oh, my life is changing everyday, in every possible way"
-The Cranberries

Blake

It's been about a week since the accident, and while on the surface, it looks like Luke is in a better place, little things still have me worried.

Like right now, he's in the shower in the ensuite bathroom so I can see him from our bed where I sit with my e-reader waiting for him so I can get ready. Tonight is the soft opening of Lit & Libations, and I should be over the moon, but I have a knot in my stomach as I stare over my screen at Luke while I pretend to read.

He is standing against the wall, head drooped, staring blankly at the water as it runs out of the showerhead.

This is what he does whenever he thinks I'm not paying attention or watching, but I'm always watching him.

Worried sick, constantly.

Frightened.

It's like my perfect boyfriend disappeared in an instant the night of the accident, like a puff of smoke vanishing. The longer it takes that boy, Adam, to recover, and the more chaotic and unpredictable the journey becomes, the more I see the pieces of Luke slipping away, unraveling, fraying at the ends. I can only hope it will improve before all that's left are fragments of who he used to be.

To make matters worse, he is distant. Cold. I don't think he means to be. I don't even think he notices, but when I try to comfort him, or talk to him, he shuts down and pretends it's all ok. Then the second anyone else, Ty, Keith, Isa, or his parents are around, he opens up like water streaming from the faucet, free flowing. It hurts and makes me feel unsure about my place in his heart, but then he looks at me, and it all melts away, if only for a moment, I feel at peace. Even in his current state he still looks at me like I'm the only one who matters.

"B, I am so fucking proud of you." He beams, turning off the water. "You are officially a business owner."

"Thanks, babe." I stand and peel off my clothes as I make my way to the shower. "Why the sudden change?"

When the last article of clothing has dropped to the floor, Luke comes up behind me, kisses my neck and wraps an arm around my body, pulling me close. "Today snuck up on me, but I've been proud of you every step of the way."

He moves my hair and continues kissing my neck. I sink into his touch, wanting it so much, but I'm running late.

"Not right now, babe. You took a little longer than usual to take a shower, and I have to be there in an hour to get everything set up." I slide out from his grip and turn on the water.

He offers me one more kiss on the cheek and a soft smile. "I'm sorry, babe. This situation has made me such a mess. I haven't even helped you get this all ready. I'll go load the car, you get ready, and I'll drive you there."

"That would be amazing." I chose not to acknowledge his comment. We both know how he has been. I know he is not doing it on purpose, so there is no sense in making him feel any worse than he already does.

I finish getting ready and take one last look in the mirror before I head downstairs. The black leather pants I am wearing are the perfect contrast to the emerald, sheer knit top highlighting the intricate details of the black bustier laying underneath. Emerald is my new favorite color to wear after visiting Lily. It enhances the red hues in my hair and complements the bold red I love to paint my lips. I was going to wear a more practical shoe, but being practical in what I wear has never been me, so I pulled out my black heels with red bottoms, that I splurged on a few years back, to pack a little punch.

My hair is down, curled to perfection, but I know once I move around I'll want it off my neck, so I grab my gold claw clip and head to the living room where Luke is packing up the last of the refreshments.

He looks up and stares at me, mouth agape. "B, wow. I um, I am really fucking glad you are my girl and I get to bring you home tonight. It will keep me from running to the bathroom to jerk off in the middle of your party," he admires me with a wink.

I smile, this is the first glimpse I've had of my man in far too long, so I grant myself permission to revel in it. I walk over, place my hand on his chest, and softly press my lips to his. When I pull away, not wanting to lose myself in the kiss before we leave, I make a sultry promise, "Well, if you behave yourself, I'll reward you for your efforts of avoiding self pleasure."

"Nope, I'll meet you there. I have to, um, I have some shit to take care of," he jokes, pulling away.

"Nice try! You promised you'd help me, and we're almost late," I laugh.

"Fine," Luke smirks with a fake pout and doe eyes. "But if I only last a few seconds, that's on you."

Man, it feels so good to have a glimpse of him back.

Luke and I set up the decorations, pre-making trays of the signature drink of the night, Prose Paloma.

We also made gift bags for all the guests. Sleek black bags filled with mini bottles of Tequila, small mixers and a recipe card so they can make the featured drink at home; a custom glass, to bring in when they visit for one free drink per visit; a QR code for the 90s playlist we have filling the speakers tonight; and little L&L stickers. The bag, of course, is topped off with sparkly red tissue paper, and a card with each person's name, sealed with a bright red kiss.

We worked tirelessly to set up all the hors d'oeuvres and sip stations where everyone can sample the drinks on the menu.

I have hired a small staff of mixologists, waitstaff, and bookstore attendants. By small, I mean there are 6 of us, including me. My manager, Amari, a girl I worked with at the bar, has had a huge hand in all the behind the scenes details for this evening. I needed someone who could be in charge should I not be able to be here, and I trust her immensely. I have hired just enough employees for two different shift rotations so they all have ample time off. However, it was imperative to me they be a part of the festivities and celebrate the opening rather than work it, so I designed every detail of the night to be 100% self-serve. I even set up a self checkout system using a QR code for the books people may want to purchase, a safe choice reserved for close family and friends only.

The party has been in full swing for about an hour and every detail is perfect.

"Blake, this is the most amazing night. I am so proud of you. Who the hell would have thought working for 'king prick bag' would have led to all this?" Ana jokes marveling at the space.

"Right." I take a sip of my drink and catch Luke's eye from across the room. Adam had a good day yesterday, so he seems extra chipper today. I think the light at the end of the tunnel is glowing, and it's just what he needs to get out of his funk.

"How are things with you two?" Ana asks, sipping her sparkling water. She is expecting baby number two soon.

"Great, he's… Ana, he is fucking dirty." I laugh. "I would have never expected the shit that comes out of his mouth."

"Yeah well, seems to have gotten you out of your funk thinking you had to be all wholesome and shit." She laughs.

"I didn't think I could be curious and explore my sexuality and have a relationship at the same time. I thought it made me look like the one-night stand type, not the take home to mom type."

"Well, you love one-night stands more than most, but I think to him you were always the exception. Plus, his mom already loved you, hoe and all," she teases, bumping me with her hip, her huge knockers catching my eye.

"Man, I forgot how hot you are when you're pregnant. And by the way, Knox keeps eye fucking you, so he must think so too," I chuckle, pointing to Knox, who is staring at Ana with a smoldering look on his face, like her appearance is searing his insides.

"Yeah, I think he's enjoying every second this time. Making up for what he missed with Riker." I can tell by her expression the memories are still a little painful.

I clear my throat, not knowing how to respond. "Yeah, well, you better go get him a cold drink before he gets so hot he can't stand up, if you know what I mean." I wiggle my eyebrows and laugh.

I grab a glass of water off the tray beside me and turn to address the room. I clank a cocktail fork on the glass to call everyone's attention.

"Thank you all so much! I am not sure I could have made the leap to do this withou-"

The bell on the door chimes and when I look back up; I see Cash.

What in the actual fuck is he doing here?

I try to shake off his presence and continue, "Sorry, Everyone here plays-"

He is holding the door open and from somewhere behind him, walks April. Leading her inside, he caresses the small of her back. He leans down and whispers something in her ear, and she looks at him with a look I have never seen before.

My heart pounds, and I question everything.

Everything I see unfolding in front of me.

Everything I know about my best friend and the current state of our relationship.

Exactly how mad she is at me.

Everything.

April wouldn't. She knows how much I fucking hate him. She knows every fucking thing that happened between the two of us. I confided in her.

As she walks through the door, he keeps contact with her and when she doesn't pull away, my blood runs cold.

Attempting to regain my composure I continue, "Everyone has played such an important role in making this happen. Cheers." I raise my glass, cutting my speech short.

He is not her fucking date, is he? There is no way.

As the two of them get farther into the light, I notice he is wearing gym clothes. He couldn't even get fucking dressed up for the occasion?

None of this is adding up.

I just stand there frozen in my place. My emotions run wild–hurt, mad, betrayed–name it and I'm feeling it. April notices the second she makes eye contact with me from across the room. She makes her way towards me, but Knox and Ana intercept, both of whom have no fucking clue about my hate for this man.

Everything around me turns to slow motion as I try to cool my nerves and regain perspective. April would never do this, no matter how mad she was at me. This is not what it seems.

Everything slows. Everything goes silent. All I can focus on is my attempt to figure out what the fuck is going on.

I watch Ana hug April. Then Cash. Knox hands something small to Cash, as if he knew he was coming. Cash tries to protest whatever is in his hand. Knox insists he take it. Luke punches Cash in the face.

Fuck. Luke PUNCHES CASH IN THE FACE.

Something inside me snaps and the silent slow-motion picture I was watching bursts to life.

Luke's beer goes flying.

I'm crazy, right? No? Luke made the same assumption. No… no way. A small sob threatens to break through as I stare in horror.

"What the fuck was that for?" Cash yells, holding his chin.

Knox steps in between Luke and Cash, placing one arm between them, confusion etched across his face. With his other hand, he nudges Ana back, and looks at April.

"Get her the fuck away from here," he demands, gesturing for April to move Ana away from the fight.

"How fucking dare you, you fucking piece of shit!" Luke yells, reaching for Cash. "You fucking belittled her to your friend, made her feel like she was not fucking worthy of love, shattering the most precious thing in the world. You had pure fucking perfection in your hands and you fucking treated it like trash, and then you had the fucking nerve to call her a bitch." He is clearly being precise with his words right now, careful not to mention my name. "And now you have the fucking audacity to show up here with my little sister! She is not a fucking toy to play with Cash, your next fucking conquest." Luke reaches out and punches Cash again around Knox's head. This time, somehow, the punch lands a little harder and draws blood on Cash's lip.

I can't even move to break it up. I'm stunned and motionless.

"Knock it the fuck off. Both of you!" Knox yells. He grabs Cash by the shirt and pushes him towards the door. "What the fuck is he talking about, Cash?" he continues under his breath as they make their way outside.

"I have no fucking clue," he responds as they exit the front door.

I look over, and Luke is whispering something in a hushed yell at April. I make my way over to tell them to leave, to take it somewhere else, but it's no use. Everyone is already staring and caught up in the drama.

Embarrassment sinks in, and I think that is crueler than the shame.

Well Fuck...

"Come and bring back my smile
Come and take these tears away"
-Toni Braxton

Blake

To say last night didn't go as planned is an understatement.

I'm not really sure April is actually dating Cash, but I'm having a hard time reconciling what my eyes saw and what my heart believes.

I've been laying here in bed awake for the last hour mindlessly scrolling my phone while I replay every detail trying to unravel the truth from what I believe, but they are so intertwined at this point I can't tell them apart.

Every time I close my eyes, all I see are faces staring at me, mouths agape as Luke punches Cash. Amari rushed over to me asking what she should do. The rest of the girls scurried around picking up trash and started putting things away.

Luke's parents stood motionless, like me. Frozen, trying to take in the shitshow unfolding in front of us.

Ana's eyes were darting frantically between me and April.

The thoughts make my stomach turn. I close Instagram as a text comes through.

Ana: Ready to talk?

I don't even respond. I just hit her contact on my phone, waiting for it to ring. She picks up before the first ring can even finish.

"First, are you ok?" she asks.

"Yes."

"What the fuck was that about? Blake, why didn't you tell me something happened?" she wonders, sounding a little desperate for answers.

"Him and Knox are boys. I didn't want to make shit weird," I explain.

"Well, we're girls, and I would have killed him. And-you failed. Shit got weird anyway."

"I know." A long exhale punctuates my mood. "I knew you would kill him, and as much as I hate him, I didn't want you to go to jail, pregnant no less, over some shitbag. No one wants to have a baby in prison, Ana."

"I could do it." Those are her only words. Her silence stretches, waiting for me to unload all of my secrets.

"We hooked up after your wedding. He got weird and left abruptly afterwards. He said some douchey shit before we hooked up about *not being here for a long time, just a good time*. I should have known right then and there, but was pussy blind." Before I continue, I take a long breath again, "I opted for a late checkout to avoid the walk of shame the next morning, and when I got to breakfast, he was behind me talking shit to some guy. I just wanted what you have so badly. I thought he was the right guy. It's ridiculous and I'm ashamed of myself-I know better. I swore off guys, thinking I was the problem. Thinking I need to be different in order to be worthy of love. My guard was up with Luke at first, and he knew it. When I told him why I was so guarded, he lost his shit. I made him promise to leave it alone, and then he saw Cash with April and lost his shit all over again." I let out an enormous sigh.

Ana is silent for a few seconds and then finally responds, "That's a lot. Ok. Let me make sure I've got this straight: aching pussy equals pussy blind, which equals hook up with a douchebag who says fucking douchey shit. Then turns into you feeling bad about yourself and Luke going all primal on his ass over it because now he's moving in on his sister."

"Pretty much," I confirm

"Wow. I can't believe he's so different from the boy next door persona he gives off in public," she adds.

"Right! I was surprised too."

"Knox insists he's a good guy. He insists there has to be more to the story with April, but if you hate him, then I fucking hate him too!" she firmly promises.

"Thanks. Shit was already so bad between April and I, and now-" my voice breaks.

"For what it's worth, I think you need to talk to April."

Ana and I talk for a while longer and she spends the rest of the conversation trying to reassure me it wasn't as bad as I think it was.

I hear Riker come running into the room asking for breakfast so we hang up, promising a lunch date soon. I lay my phone on the bed and sigh. Not knowing how to make any of this better.

I feel the bed next to me dip, and a soft caress of Luke's hand across my arm.

"Morning baby."

I take a sharp breath, turning slightly to face him, my words already on the tip of my tongue.

But then I freeze, everything I've been holding back suddenly weighs heavier than I can speak.

"I–"

And just like that, the moment shatters, leaving me unsure if I even want to say it.

"**M**ORNING," SHE REPLIES BACK as she stands from the bed and walks to the shower. She silently turns on the water, undresses, and throws her hair up in a clip.

I sit on the end of the bed and watch her intently as she shaves her legs, washes her body and face. As she glides the loofah across her skin, I can't help but wish I was the fucking loofah. What I wouldn't give to touch her right now.

When she steps out of the shower and starts to dry her skin, I stand and inch my way into the bathroom, tail between my legs.

"B, I'm really sorry. I shouldn't have-"

"No, you shouldn't have, Luke," she interrupts. "You literally walked up and punched him in front of all the people I invited to celebrate my important night with me."

"I was trying to defend you-protect you," I explain.

"Luke, I don't need you to protect me or defend my honor. I can defend myself," she argues.

"What exactly do you need me for? Orgasms?"

She shakes her head, anger sliding across her face like water cascading back off the shore on the sand. "I don't need you for orgasms either," she snarls.

"I broke all your toys, B. So you kinda do." As if my weak argument is worth anything.

"I have a fucking hand, Luke," she fires back.

"Answer my question. What do you need me for?" I insist.

"Luke, I don't *need* you for a goddamn thing. I wan-"

"Nothing right," I interject before she can finish her sentence, "except a place to live for free so you can afford your bar."

Fuck.

I don't mean them, but I can't stop the words from tumbling out of my mouth, and the look crossing her face guts me.

"Baby, no, no, no, you know I don't mean- I'm sorry. Please forget what I said."

"I told you before I moved in here, I can take care of myself," she states unwaveringly as she moves to the bedroom.

"Baby, please," I plead

She silently gets dressed, throws clothes on in a fury.

"Blake, let's talk," I beg.

She packs a bag, blindly throwing everything inside without the precision or care she usually possesses.

I try to pull the bag from her grip, begging her to look at me for just a second. If she would just look at me, she would see how much I truly love her. Instead, she opens the front door and storms out.

I fall apart on the floor. What did I just do?

After a few hours, I decided space is the only thing that is going to make this better. We both need time to digest this fight, and she needs time to cool off.

"Hey, mom," I whisper when my mom calls me back. I called an hour ago, but she didn't answer.

"Still rough over there? Last night was a doozy." She's trying to ease the tension.

"How can you be so nonchalant about this?" I ask.

"Luke, you and B love each other. You have for a while now. It's been plain as day, staring everyone in the face. I told your dad just as much not long after you married *that* girl."

"Noel?" I ask, rolling my eyes,

She bluntly ignores me. "I told him there was no way your marriage would last. You were in love with Blake." She pauses before she continues, "Relationships hit bumps. This is your first big fight. It will pass."

"Mom, I told her the only thing she needs from me is a free place to live." I shake my head in disapproval.

"Okay, so this is your first fuck up," she verifies. "Luke, honestly, that was the dumbest thing you could have said," she scolds.

"I know, I don't mean it," I murmur in regret.

"I know." She takes another long breath. "So does she."

"I think we need a little space. Emotions are too high right now. Can I come stay there for a few days?" I ask.

"Yes, but not too long. You are not running from this. You need to fix it," she encourages.

I head out to get Blake some coffee and a bagel. I know she doesn't eat when she's upset, and she is moody when she doesn't eat. She and the girls have a lot to do in the next few days before L&L opens to the public.

When I walk into the bar, I hear them having a meeting in the back. I grab a napkin and a pen from behind the bar and leave a brief note next to the coffee and bagel.

I look one more time towards the back room, hoping to get a glimpse of my girl before I leave, but when I don't, I turn towards the door and head to my parents' house.

Shit, Shit, Shit...

"Have you ever needed somethin' so bad
You can't sleep at night?"
-Brandy

Blake

I SHOULD BE SLEEPING.

I'm supposed to be thrilled, L&L is officially open. I should be a lot of things, but right now, all I am is sad.

Sad April and I are at odds.

Sad that the soft opening of L&L fell apart.

Sad that the man I love is not here in our bed with me, but miles away at his parents' house.

Most of all, I'm sad I prefer not to be with him right now.

There are a million different ways I could describe my feelings as I lay here and stare at the ceiling, but tonight, there is no better word than sad.

I'm used to not getting the things I want, and most times growing up, not even getting the things I needed. I spent many nights alone growing up, little to no food in the house, no detergent to clean my clothes because mom was too busy getting busy with any man who would pay her attention. That's why I spent so much time with April and her family. So, this feeling of disappointment rolling around inside me that things are not the way I want, is all too familiar.

Maggie has called me several times. She also sent a few texts, but I just can't bring myself to respond. She is the best maternal figure I have had in my life, yet, in a lot of ways, I'm a product of my upbringing, despite her positive influence in my most crucial years.

I forget to eat when I'm in a funk, and retreat to my turtle shell when I'm overwhelmed, overworked, or sad. I try to self-soothe because it's my best defense against the pressures, disappointments, and realities of the cruel world outside, lurking in the shadows of seemingly mundane moments.

Monotony is the bane of my existence. I function best at a busy, nonstop pace. When things are quiet, simple, and calm, my brain takes over.

I roll over and look at the clock, it's 2:52 am. I started getting ready for bed at 10:16. Got in the shower, dried my hair, put on my nightly skin care regimen, and finally settled in bed to watch tv at 11:34. I have been laying here pretending to watch tv ever since. It's been a little over a week, but I can't find a rhythm, or balance. I have lived on my own for most of my life, or at least been alone at night, but Luke's absence in our bed, his bed, is gaping, the vortex of this cold void pulling me under. I sink further into the sad abyss each night, but I also need the space.

Luke: Goodnight, B. Sweet dreams.

I stare down at Luke's text. It comes like clockwork every night, somewhere between 9:00 and 10:00. It's the one thing I both look forward to and dread each night. I miss him like crazy, and I know we need to talk. The texts make me feel so loved despite the distance, but the dread of what to say, how to respond, is consuming. I miss him, and I want him to know it, but the things that have happened are not ok, and I need him to understand that too. But are they worth potentially losing each other over?

No.

I don't know how to move forward, but I don't know how to exist like this either.

I love him with all my heart, and I know he loves me too, but what if April is right? What if she's been right all along? What if we aren't ready, and we rushed into things and are truly not prepared for something like this? Sometimes the path ahead is clearer when you are on the outskirts. Maybe she saw the warning signs while the dense underbrush of love, of lust, obstructed our view.

I lay here feeling like I'm a tilt-a-whirl, unable to make out the direction I am heading. Luke and I have been avoiding our feelings in the private solace of our own minds for years. We are soulmates and lovers, not a product of lust and impulse. We're not.

Shit, shit, shit, we're not right?

I hate the fucking mundane stillness of the night. It allows my inner demons to surface out of the shadows where they are lurking and overtake my brain.

I look back at the clock: 3:27. Deciding I sleep is not in the cards, I slide on my slippers, grab a blanket, and head to the kitchen to make some coffee.

When the coffee finishes brewing, I turn on a lamp to cast a warm glow over the room, grab a book off the shelf and read.

I reread the same line repeatedly, because I can't focus on the words sprawled across the page.

Not being able to talk myself out of it, I pick up the phone and dial Luke's number. Maybe if I leave him a message, get the words out instead of leaving them trapped in my head, unknown to even myself, I can get some goddamn sleep.

The phone rings once. "B, what's wrong? I'm on my way." I hear him fumbling around, scrambling in what I can imagine is a dark room.

"No, I don't want to see you. I just-" Taking a moment to find the words, I pause, "I just needed to hear your voice. I needed to get my words out." Nothing I am saying makes sense. I place one hand over my face and shake my head in frustration.

"Ok." He has a breathy tone, and I can hear him pulling out a chair to sit down. He remains silent on the other end. He just waits.

So do I.

We just sit in silence for what feels like an eternity while we both wait for the words to surface. After a beat, I look at the screen and see we have been, in fact, sitting in this silence for 9 minutes and 34 seconds.

"I'm sad." My heart shatters at the admission. "I'm sad that I'm sad and I don't want you here. Sad, I still need space even when I'm sad. But you are also who I need." I laugh with a little cry, broken by the void between us.

"I'm sorry, B." He doesn't push, he doesn't defend himself or try to make it right. He knows I need this space, and this-whatever this is. This is what I love about him.

We go back to being silent, and stay on the phone for a long time.

I hear a muffled voice from the speakers in the background. He's at work.

"Do you need to go?" I ask, hoping the answer is no.

"Not yet. I'm on call, so I was just resting in the on-call room. They're not paging me." I can hear the light smile in his voice.

"You should rest."

"B, being on the phone listening to your breath is the most rested I have been since I left." This makes a small smile tug at my lips.

We go back to being silent, listening to the steady beat of each other's breath. The melody lulls me into a peaceful sleep.

Luke

I DRIFTED IN AND out of the most peaceful broken sleep I have ever experienced, sitting on the phone with my B. I was so at peace, and wanting to just hear her breath, and have her in any way I can.

I got a page at 5:15. Not wanting to wake her, I sent her a text letting her know I was going back to work, but would think about her all day. I am not sure what last night meant, and I don't want to push or make her feel like she has to talk or not talk. I want her to come around in her own time.

I'm exhausted, but feel more relaxed, more at ease, than I have in almost a week. Before I leave work I want to check on Adam.

It's still early in the morning, only 7:15, so I don't want to wake him. I stop at the nurses' station instead. Who am I kidding? I wouldn't go in even if he was awake. I never will. He doesn't even know I check on him. Lucy, the charge nurse, looks at me with a big smile as I approach. She knows exactly why I'm here.

"Why the smile?" I ask, taken slightly off guard. She rarely smiles. She's distant. Cold, most likely a front to make her job bearable. Working with critical patients can take a toll on you after a while.

"They moved him out of the ICU last night. You're officially on the wrong floor, Doc." She smiles, and it's so contagious I find a smile spreading across my face as well.

"That's great. Great news." I am overjoyed.

Neither one of us is bubbly. There is no need for more conversation. I give her a wave and head to the elevator.

Thankfully, the ride down the elevator is quick. I can't wait to get home. The doors slide open and the smell of coffee from the cart invades my senses. I rarely drink coffee at the end of an overnight shift, but today, I got little sleep, and I know feeling rested and being rested are two very different things. I need a little pick me up for the drive home-my temporary home, not the one where my girl is.

The barista hands me my cup, and when I turn around to leave I come face to face with Cash. His shoulders tense, and I follow in response. For a second, we exchange silent stares, heavy and unspoken, as we continue in each other's direction.

He takes a rugged breath as we pass each other, and I hear a faint whisper as our shoulders brush. "I'm not after her."

I pause. "No, you don't have to be. You have her. Right?" He just shakes his head and turns in the direction he was going. "You better not hurt her. She's my sister Cash," I yell after him, but he doesn't acknowledge my words.

After he takes a few more steps, he turns on his heels and heads back in my direction. He waits until he gets close enough to whisper before he speaks, "Listen, what you think you saw with April is too much to unpack right now, but I know Blake hates me, and by default you do, too. But the shitty fucking thing is, she hates me for no fucking reason."

"No reason? What a joke." He gauges my expression, which is flat. When he speaks, this time, it's above the hushed whisper he previously spoke with, clearly a little more confident.

"Luke, I'm not fucking joking. I don't have any idea why she's so pissed. Enlighten me."

He waits, and I realize he means it. He has no idea why she's so upset with him.

"She said the morning after you hooked up she overheard you talking shit about her not being game day material or some shit." I roll my eyes. "What does that even fucking mean?"

He stares at me thoughtfully for a moment, clearly replaying that encounter in his head. "Betty!" Something clearly dawns on him. "I was talking about the new bat I bought, Luke. Who the hell would refer to a woman like that?" he questions.

"Who refers to their bat like a woman?" I probe.

"Same kind of guys who name their cars and boats."

Fair.

"What about when you called her a fucking bitch at the hospital?" I ask.

"What? I di-" His face morphs into a painful grimace. "I hit my fucking hand on the stupid metal rail between the doors, and it hurt like a bitch. Look," he says, holding out his hand. I stare at the faint yellow and green evidence of an old bruise across his knuckles.

"Listen, I'm over all the demands of being a professional athlete, the expectations women hold, and I was ready to connect with someone. I owe her an explanation and I hate that she's been feeling like this. I mean, it explains a lot about how she's acted towards me, but I don't think she will hear it. So please, you're my only chance. I'm glad she found you, Luke. At first I was hoping you were just a fling; I even tried to convince her it could be. I wanted a shot, but Knox is one of my best friends. He's important to me, and I know Blake is one of Ana's best friends. What Ana thinks is important to me, and right now, she thinks I am a giant shit bag."

"Go on," I sigh, not wanting to engage in this conversation. Not sure I even believe a word coming out of his mouth.

"I'd never had a one-night stand before, so I hurried out of there because I didn't know what else to do. I was planning on getting her number from Knox after their honeymoon, but shit went sideways before I got the chance. I only knew she was upset because she stormed out of the hotel cafe, flipping me off. Now I know why, and I don't blame her. She probably thinks I'm a giant tool."

I let him ramble longer than I ever would have, surprised he wasn't more of a playboy. There was also a small part of me that also wanted to hear him out-wanted to know he didn't treat my girl like trash and thought more of her than she thinks.

"Blake is a fucking gift. I'm glad you see that, but I'm not sad you unintentionally fucked it up with her," I sneer, dripping with arrogance. "She's mine, Cash. But she won't want to hear any of this from me. Maybe you need to talk to Knox," I suggest as I walk away. "I'll talk to you later."

This is my life now, 15 steps forward and 15 steps back. While I am so fucking happy Adam is making progress, and Cash didn't disrespect my girl, the feeling is fleeting when coupled with the desperation I have to be home. Really home.

It's so Obvious

"Lost for you, I'm so lost for you
You come crash, into me"
-Dave Matthews Band

Blake

I T'S BEEN A FEW days since I called Luke. He is doing exactly what I asked, giving me space and letting me process my feelings, but fuck, part of me wishes he would forget everything I said I want and storm through the doors and reclaim me.

I've spent all morning here at L&L getting things ready for the night shift. L&L is open all day. Books and coffee by day, smut and cocktails by night.

It's become the go-to place for quite a few book club meetups. Tonight we have a busier night than usual. Three book club reservations and tomorrow morning, we have a book signing for a local author. All resulting in L&L being closed to the public for the next two days. While I hate having to close to the public, it seems to have created this exclusiveness. The few times we have had to close, the next night we find ourselves busier than before.

My biggest hesitation right now lies in the fact we have a full house reserved tonight and I can't be here. I have so much faith in Amari, she can and will handle it. I'm just sad I won't be here to see a packed house. It's my favorite sight.

Knox is finally opening a youth baseball facility he has been building from the ground up, and after all the unwavering support he and Ana have shown me, I wouldn't miss his celebration for the world. Knox didn't want a big fuss, so they only invited a few people to celebrate. I know it will be mostly baseball related friends, including Cash, so I am also planning on taking a run before I go to release some pent up energy I have so I don't rip his face off.

"Ok, I have the bar restocked, inventory done, and the girls and I are going to set up the tables for tonight," Amari reassures me as she walks out of the back.

"You are the best!" I smile. "I could not do this without you. Please take me up on my offer and take the next two days off. Please."

"Blake, I have to work tonight, anyway. You hired me as your manager. The point of having a manager is to have someone who can take care of things so you can have time off, too. Plus, I'm not leaving you high and dry when we have two private events." I inspect her expression for any hint of hesitation.

"I know, girl, but this is a big undertaking. It's the first big event we have hosted. What if something goes wrong?" The worry in my voice echoes across the bar.

"Shit will probably go wrong, Blake. It's a bar." Her joking tone does nothing to comfort me. "Listen, if we fuck up their order or take too long, I'll comp a bottle of champagne to the party. If they hate the atmosphere, they can get fucked. If they get too drunk and rowdy, the only one they can annoy is me. I'll order them a ride share when they're ready to leave using the vouchers we have in the back and send them on their way. If the bar catches on fire or floods, or heaven forbid a riot breaks out, I'll call 911 and then I'll call you so you can race down here." She snorts out a laugh.

I roll my eyes. "Ok, when you put it that way, I would be ridiculous for worrying."

"We can compromise. Tonight will be a late night, and tomorrow will be a long day. I'll take the next day off," she tries to negotiate.

"Paid," I insist.

"Paid," she repeats with a roll of her eyes.

"Who in their right mind argues with their boss over paid time off?" I question as she leaves the room.

"Have fun tonight." She waves over her shoulder and the back door closes gently behind her.

I can't take all of this. It's been too hard, so I take the moment alone as a sign to try and mend one broken relationship.

After a few rings April answers.

"Hey, B."

"Ap, I'm sorry. I should have never hid my feelings from you. I told myself, I told Luke, Ana told me more times than I can count that I should have told you before anything happened. It wasn't planned, but the writing was on the wall."

"Shit happens, B. I was just feeling more shut out than anything else." Her voice is ragged, like she might cry.

"I wasn't trying to shut you out, I was trying to avoid making you uncomfortable."

"I realize that now," she confirms.

"April, while we're talking I need to get something off my chest."

"Ok."

"You said you'd pick him, and you implied I'm not family too, but to me you are my family. You're the closest thing I have to one. I've spent holidays, birthdays, and random nights eating dinner with your family, doing all the things families do. It stung Ap."

"B," she sobs on the other line. "B, you are my family. I was so scared to lose you that I said that without thinking. The fear of the unknown was too much for me to register. I am so fucking sorry, B"

I change the call to FaceTime.

"I need to see your face." I laugh.

"Shit, B. I've missed you so much. Are you ok? I know shit went sideways, Mom said Luke's staying at their house."

I hesitate for a second, but I know I have to let her in, let her see our relationship.

"No, I'm a mess." I take a deep breath, "I love him, April."

"Then what are you guys doing?"

"He said things that hurt me, and I got pissed and left."

She laughs, "Yeah, you do that sometimes, but he shouldn't say dumb shit either. The sooner you realize this is a fight and not the end, the better off you will be."

I take a moment, the weight of her words settling in. She's right, of course. But April's the one who's always seen the bigger picture, even when I can't.

"I don't know," I whisper, my voice faltering. "It's just… so hard, you know? I want to believe things will be okay, but right now, it feels like everything's falling apart."

"You're stronger than this, B. You've made it through worse. And he's not going anywhere. Trust me."

I nod, but the uncertainty still gnaws at me. The thought of what comes next is terrifying. But maybe, just maybe, I can trust her words. Trust that what we have is worth fighting for. "Maybe you're right."

April's response gives me a reassuring little nudge, "You're gonna be okay. Go get him back, B. But don't make it too easy."

My shoulders are tense, and my feet feel like lead as I turn the corner, finishing my run. Between missing the L&L event tonight, not talking to Luke, and the thought of being in the same room as Cash all night, I'm a wreck.

What the hell do I wear tonight? Baseball facility celebration at a house doesn't really call for a night out kind of outfit. Unable to decide, I pick up my phone to call Ana. It rings a few times, and I think it's about to go to voicemail when she answers.

"Hey," her voice is loud over the music in the background.

I look at the clock, and it's only 5:30. The party isn't supposed to start for another two hours.

"Sorry, are you pre-gaming?" I ask.

"Sorry, hang on for a second. I can't hear you." She moves and I can hear her footsteps on the floor as the sound of the music fades. "Sorry, Knox is blaring music while he is setting up the tables and shit."

"Oh," I laugh. "What the hell are you wearing tonight? I don't know what to wear to this kind of event."

"Well, I don't think the leather maternity yoga jumper I have on will suit you." She chuckles. "But I have it paired with a low cut sheer top and my boots. Nothing too fancy, but I'm trying to have what little sex appeal I can for Knox."

"Shut up, Ana, you're a smoke show and based on the way he can't keep his hands off you. You'll be pregnant again soon. Better get used to pregnant sex appeal."

Knox loves Ana, and he cannot keep his hands to himself EVER. Ana brings out this primal side in him; he is not afraid to show off.

"Thanks," I can hear her smile through the phone. "Was anything I said helpful?" she asks.

"Yep, I have the perfect outfit," I respond with confidence.

"Not sure if it will change your mind about what you wear, but Luke is coming. Knox ran into him at the store. I was going to call you to give you a heads up once we had everything set up."

My skin tightens, and little goosebumps erupt all over my skin and wetness pools between my legs. My body has a mind of its own when it comes to this man.

"Actually, it does," I breathe out.

"Blake, what are you doing?" Ana asks, with clear judgment in her voice. "You have wanted him for so long, and now you have him and you're giving up? I don't understand. Well… I understand, but trust me, it's not worth it."

I know she's right. I watched her and Knox carry on for years, pining after each other, letting the little shit impede their ability to be in love.

"I don't know." The admission feels like acid. "I'm just so mad at him right now."

"Yup. You know, you can be mad at him, and still love him. You can also be mad at him and live with him. It can all happen at once, Blake. One thing I've learned over the years is that more than one thing can be true at a time, even if the ideas contradict each other. Don't be like me. Don't wait until it almost slips through your fingers to have love."

"I know." There is nothing else to say. I know she's right, and I'm not even sure how to answer her first question. What am I doing? What do I want to gain from this?

There is a loud noise from somewhere in Ana's house. "Hey, Knox is going to break something trying to set shit up on his own," she laughs. "I'll see you tonight."

"See you soon." I set down my phone and head to grab my clothes while the shower heats.

Two and a half hours later, running later than I expected, I pull up to Ana and Knox's house. Ana bought this house shortly before they got back together, and I absolutely love it. It's a small, two-bedroom ranch-style house nestled in a small neighborhood surrounded by trees as far as you can see. It is the picturesque vision of Vermont in every season, a small cottage feel, with stone and wood finishings.

I hear a bunch of people and music as I walk up the short walkway in the middle of the lawn, lined with small bushes.

"Hey," Cash's voice causes a visceral reaction in me, my stomach tightens, my jaw clenches, and for a split second I'm not sure if I want to punch him or walk away.

Deciding I don't want to mess up my look before I see Luke, I head for the door.

"Blake, I'm so incredibly sorry. There was a huge misunderstanding."

I stop and turn around, only to be met with the most genuine gaze.

"I know I left abruptly that night. I saw it on your face. But I'd never hooked up with anyone outside of a relationship, and I didn't know what to do." He looks down at his feet, kicking a rock back and forth. "I know, not quite the star athlete persona people are used to. But I had a great time, Blake. I planned on getting your number from Knox after the honeymoon."

"Ok. That doesn't explain you talking shit the next morning," I retort.

"Fuck, this is embarrassing. I was talking with my buddy about a bat I just bought. I named her Betty, it's a baseball thing." He shakes his head. "I bought it on a whim, because it was the hot new thing, and I was hitting like shit with it. I didn't know you overheard that, and I can see how it must have sounded, but Blake, I promise it was taken out of context. I would never talk about you, or anyone for that matter, like that."

I break out in uncontrollable laughter.

"Are you serious? A bat?" I try to catch my breath. "What about the day in the hospital?"

"Bad timing. I hit my hand of the fucking door right before you came around the corner." He offers me a shy smile. "Blake, the only one questioning your worth, was you. Trust me, you're one of a kind, and Luke is so lucky to have you."

"Thank you for the apology. I appreciate it. I'm sorry I caused all this drama for you."

"It will pass. I'm glad I ran into you before I left."

"Where are you going?" I ask.

"Just stopped by to give Knox my congrats. I have a flight back to San Diego. I'll be back in a few weeks." He takes a step closer now that it's clear I'm not likely to punch him.

"May I?" he asks, gesturing for a hug.

"Of course."

He gives me a quick hug before he leaves, and I'm actually glad I ran into him. It's like a weight has been lifted.

I knock, but realize they will never hear it over all the noise and make my way inside. The living room is full of people I don't recognize, but I spot Knox in the corner by the fireplace, talking to an older gentleman.

I smile and wave, offering him a silent hello as I make my way to the kitchen. The island in the center has basic party food alongside fancy hors d'oeuvres, and various bottles of wine, whisky, gin, and tequila line the counters. I scan the room for Ana, and let's be honest, for Luke, but don't spot either of them.

Deciding I need help to calm my nerves, I grab a glass and pour myself a generous serving of Tempranillo.

"She is nothing I would have expected. Knox is delicious," a bleach blond next to me tells the woman she is talking to. Both of their backs to me as they talk in hushed whispers.

"Right? I was expecting tall, fake boobs. You know someone who wears a lot of makeup, makes a statement on his arm. The way he talks about her, you'd think she was pure perfection."

I roll my eyes. I hate women like this.

The other woman's husband, judging by the band on his ring finger, leans in to kiss her cheek. While doing so, he grabs a cracker and keeps walking towards the living room where Knox is. Clearly, the kiss was a courtesy when what he actually wanted was a snack, and not the fun kind.

"If Knox was who I came home to every night, I'd put in a little more effort. I wouldn't want him to wander," the first woman continues. "All the moms are waiting for the green light, so they can make a move. Especially the single ones." She laughs.

Her friend smiles, "You are one of those single moms."

"Then I speak from experience," the first woman's smug voice causes my eyes to narrow into slits as I try to burn daggers through the back of her head.

I watch as they both go silent and I follow their gaze to Ana, coming out of Riker's bedroom. She is absolutely glowing, and these two women are not the only ones who notice. I glance in Knox's direction who is mid conversation, but as if her presence is a magnetic pull, without looking in her direction, he quickly finishes his conversation moving towards her. He makes his way over to her, bites his lip ring and wraps his arms around her. As he pulls her into his chest, he peppers her with kisses, causing her to giggle.

"Not sure she has to work very hard to keep him around," the married woman states with a slight swoon to her voice. "He seems pretty consumed by her. I would give my left tit to have my husband look at me the way he looks at her. Odds are you need to give up on the obsession and move on."

The bleach blond perks up. "Oh, did you see the eye candy in the garage? He was getting a beer out of the cooler and the veins on those tattooed forearms were so hot. Think he's single?"

Now I perk up, instantly knowing she is talking about Luke, and fuck no, he is not single.

"He looked like he was by himself. Shoot your shot if nothing else, oh, there he is," the married woman cuts out, hitting her friend on the arm.

I glance up at the door across the kitchen, only to lock eyes with my man. Fuck, he is hot. He is wearing a black button up with the sleeves rolled up. I notice how perfect his hair sits, and the recent trim of his beard. However, my attention quickly shifts to the look he gives me. It's dark, not one I usually garnish from him.

"Holy fuck, he's staring in this direction like he wants to destroy someone. I bet he could manhandle you in bed," the married woman continues.

You have no fucking clue.

I swallow, my mouth running dry as he stalks in my direction and I'm not sure if I should be nervous this is the end of us based on his face or if I should put my knuckles up ready to fight, but I know for sure my panties are soaking wet based on the aching pulse between my legs.

"Do I look ok?" the blonde in front of me asks her friend as Luke approaches, mere feet away.

Hot is all her friend gets out before Luke places a hand on the blonde's shoulder cutting her off.

"Excuse me," he cuts in with urgency, pushing between them staring daggers at me. I hear a faint scoff from the two women, but can't focus too much attention on it. Fuck. He's… I don't know what he is. My heart is pounding and my hands are clammy. "What are you trying to do, B?"

My eyebrow raises, not knowing what in the hell he is talking about. "I'm drinking wine, trying to calm my nerves," I reveal honestly, inhaling his mint and cedar scent, and it makes my toes curl in my boots. His hand slips beneath the crop top I am wearing as he places a hand on my waist and the sensation of his skin on mine causes a small whimper to leave my mouth.

"Fuck," he smolders, leaning down to whisper in my ear, only it's not a whisper. "I'm done. Done missing your smell, the feel of you wrapped in my arms, of your warm skin against mine in our fucking bed, B. Most of all I'm done missing your taste on my tongue, and then you walk in here like this, making a sexy little noise. I have nothing left, B. Fucking put me out of my misery."

The words hang in the air between us, heavy and raw, and for a moment, all I can do is stare at him, heart racing, mouth dry.

I could walk away. I could make this easier for both of us.

But the weight of what he's asking… of what we both want…

I don't know if I have the strength to say no.

Luke

I SAW A flash of red behind two women in the kitchen, and instantly knew it's her.

She's looking at her wineglass and I can tell by her body language she is straining to hear whatever the women in the way of my fucking view of her are saying. As if summoning my desire, the women turned towards each other and as they parted, the gates to heaven opened behind them. I got a full glimpse of B, and I went dark with desire. I stalk towards her in calculated motions, lightly pushing the women aside, begging my dick to stay down. The amount of focus and control I have to exert to keep my dick from going hard is unbearable.

As she talks the rise and fall of her chest is thick with desire. Her red locks flowing in loose curls running down her arms and chest, outlining the swell of her breasts perfectly, and by the sudden peak of her nipples, I can tell she's braless, making my quest even more difficult.

There she is standing here, legs crossed, propped up against the counter, full of attitude. She is wearing a dark gray, cropped graphic t-shirt, and it hits just above the band of her knit black skirt, showing just enough skin. The fitted skirt shows off every delicious curve of her hips. I bet her ass looks fucking amazing. As my eyes roam down her body, I see another sliver of skin between the bottom of her skirt and the top of the black heeled boots she is wearing. To top off the look, she painted her lips signature red, plump and delicious. I want to suck her full bottom lip into my mouth.

After I bare my heart to Blake, she just stands there mouth agape.

She swallows, and the vision of her throat constricting before me makes my desire grow even harder to contain.

"I don't know what to say, Luke," she finally murmurs after a beat.

"Say you knew I would be here, and you put this on for me, tell me your pebbled nipples are hard for me, and your thighs are slick from my proximity and that's why you keep shifting your weight back and forth, you're trying to find some friction. Tell me how fucking badly you want me to take you home, B."

"Holy fuck-that is so fucking hot," a voice whispers behind me, and I realize we still have an audience. Before Blake can answer, my darkest desires scatter due to the interruption. I have to get her out of here.

"Damn, you look hot. Aren't you glad I told her you'd be here, Luke?" Ana's eyes are glistening mischievously as she pulls Blake into a hug.

I nod in agreement, not allowing my eyes to leave Blake's face.

Knox's hand clasps my shoulder. "Dude, I know that look." He looks at Ana and clears his throat. "I've had that look more times than I can count. Let's grab a beer." He pulls me away from Blake.

"What look?" Ana laughs.

"The look of feral desire to bend you over the kitchen counter and fuck you until you can't walk tomorrow," Knox bends down and speaks in Ana's ear, not really giving a shit who hears. Knox is the guy who wants everyone to know Ana is his. I feel that.

The two women are still shamelessly watching, eyes wide. My guess is they have a thing for Knox, and his mouth just amplified their desires and solidified the fact he is off the market, clearly strategic.

He pulls me a few feet away and hands me a beer.

"Why are you looking at her like you want to maul her?" he asks with a laugh.

My eyes are still on Blake. "I have been sleeping on my parents' couch since the opening, and look at her. I can't do it anymore." Suddenly, for reasons I can't explain, I snap my attention to Knox and ask in a panic, "Is Cash here?"

"No, he flew back home. Why?" he asks, looking puzzled.

"I need to make things right with Blake, and I will be taking her home tonight. I can't have him cock blocking me by making her pissed."

Knox just laughs. "You know, all of this shit between him and Blake is a huge misunderstanding."

"I know. He told me that the other day at work. Doesn't mean I'm ok with him moving in on April." I keep my gaze fixed on Blake as I speak, as if she'll vanish if I look away.

"Yeah, I'm not sure what that's about, but I'll get it out of him eventually. Listen, I know you have all kinds of pent up shit with Blake, but Ana is driving me fucking wild tonight. Apparently I have a pregnancy kink, and she is fucking hot as fuck. I'll have her help me get more plates, I'll steal a kiss or two, and you can shoot your shot with Blake, just take her home before shit gets heated." Knox winks.

I give him a curt nod, knowing he has nothing to worry about. The things I will do to Blake are not things anyone else gets to bear witness to.

I watch as Knox walks up behind Ana, kisses her neck and pulls her out the back door, leaving all their guests to themselves, and the two women in the kitchen speechless.

"Where is Knox?" some guy walks up and asks the two women. "We are supposed to talk about the upcoming camp for the boys."

"He's busy," she points, her voice dripping with disdain.

"Oh, well, I can go grab him. You know, save him from having to entertain people," he answers thoughtlessly, taking a step towards the door.

She puts her hand out in front of him to stop him. "Not sure he wants you to interrupt him at the moment," she scoffs.

"Yeah," the other chick rolls her eyes, clearly jealous.

"Nice," the guy reacts by high fiving some other fucking douchebag who followed him over.

I listen to this exchange while I make my way back over to Blake as she refills her wine. I grab the glass out of her hand and set it on the counter. "Nope. You had one giant ass glass already, Blake, I don't want you too drunk when I take you home, it will spoil all the delicious plans I have. Text Ana and tell her good night," I request with a hint of dominance in my voice, knowing as the words leave my lips, they will ruffle her feathers.

"Get fucked Luke," she responds with a defiant little smirk and a slight laugh in her tone. With a delicate touch, she picks up the glass, the condensation clinging to its surface, and takes a long, slow sip.

"Trying to, baby, and I want you to have a clear fucking head when I sink inside you. We're done playing this fucking game."

"What fucking game is that, Luke? Me being pissed at you is a game?"

"Not at all. But, we both know this is not the end of us. It's a fight. We can fight at home. The game I'm referring to is us wasting our time being apart, like two people who have succumbed to the fact they are over, instead of making up and making love. We are not over, Blake. I let you go once without you even knowing it. I stayed married to someone else when all I wanted was you. This time, B, I'm not letting you go." I claim her lips, crashing them to mine.

When we finally pull apart, she stares into my eyes, coated in desire.

"Take me home," she demands breathlessly, snaking her hand behind my neck and pulling me in closer to her. "I think I want to see how we make up."

"I'll bring you back to your car tomorrow. Leave the keys for Knox in case he needs to move it." I pull her towards the door, peering at her perfect smile over my shoulder.

She pauses and looks at the two women as we pass. "When Mrs. Reed comes back, can you let her know Blake left with Luke, and thank her for a lovely party?" She doesn't wait for their response. She quickly continues walking towards the door, moving past me, her ass swaying in perfect rhythm.

I glance at the two women who watch her, seething with envy, and then settle my attention back on Blake.

We were silent the entire drive home. I was afraid to open my mouth, knowing it would cause me to pull over on the side of the road to take her. My dick was pressing against my jeans so hard I might have a zipper impression when it finally gets free. Blake sat next to me in the passenger seat, eyes fixed on the road ahead. The second I parked my car, she jumped out, not even waiting for me to turn off the ignition.

Worried she might peel her clothes off before I joined her, I ran behind her, readjusting my dick in the elevator to the apartment.

Now, I'm fumbling with the keys, unable to get this fucking door to open.

"Luke," she urges impatiently. "What the hell is your deal? It's a lock you have opened thousands of times before."

"I'm not usually distracted by you when I try to open it." I can hear the strain in my voice, my patience paper-thin.

She reaches over and grabs the key out of my hand, smoothly unlocks it and pushes the door open, stepping inside. We barely make it in far enough for the door to close behind us before she pushes me against it, hands in my hair and pressing her body against mine.

"Luke." It's one simple word.

"Baby, I need you. I can't worship you the way I want to, ok? Is that ok?" I ask.

"Luke, I have been rubbing my legs together for over an hour. I need you to make it better, please."

I spin her around and pin her against the door with her hands above her head. "You leave these here. Do you hear me?"

She nods her head in response as I bend down and lift her skirt so I can retrieve her panties. When my hands slide over her hips, I stop, glaring up at her.

"Where the fuck are your panties, Blake?"

"I had panty lines." She shrugs.

"Do you know how many guys were eyeing you tonight? They probably all knew you were not wearing panties."

"I doubt it." She runs her hands through my hair.

"Why?" I ask, placing her hands back where I left them with a hint of a warning in my gaze.

"Luke, baby, I need you to focus on the task at hand, making my pussy feel better. I promise you, none of them noticed I was missing panties. There was not a single person there eyeing my ass more than you were, and you didn't notice. So, please, shut the fuck up and get to work." She smiles, wiggling her brows.

I work my way up her leg, peppering it with kisses in my wake. When I get to the apex of her thighs, they are slick, coated with her arousal. The smell is intoxicating.

I press my thumb to her clit and watch as she shudders slightly, her head falling back against the door and her eyes roll back in her head.

"Yes," she pants.

I work her to the edge of release before pulling away. This time when her hands fall I allow it.

I stand up and unbutton my pants, then unzip them, allowing my dick to come free, a small piece of release I have been desperately needing.

I pick her up and wrap her legs around me as I walk her to the kitchen counter. I set her down and spin her so she's pressing her ass against me. Sliding my hand around her neck, I pull her ear close to me. "Bend over."

She does, and the swell of her ass in the moonlight filtering through the window is a sight I will burn into my memory forever. I pull my cock out and line it up with her slit. Wetness is already coating my tip as I pause, pulling away for a second.

Her protest is futile in the dark apartment.

"Luke," she groans.

I walk over to the freezer and try to sneakily fill a cup with ice. When I walk back behind Blake, I take one of the ice cubes I had hidden in my hand and slide my hand up her shirt and run the cold cube over the peaks of her nipples beneath. The hiss that leaves her mouth is beautiful. With my other hand, I line myself back up to her entrance and slide inside in one quick motion. Simultaneously, I take my hand from her breast and slide the ice cube beneath the band of her skirt and run it over her clit, making slow circles.

She shudders beneath my touch. "Luke."

I take advantage of the extra slickness and pump in and out of her at a rapid pace, banging her hips into the counter with each thrust.

"Fuck, I'm going to bruise your hips." I pull back slightly.

"Luke, fuck me right now. If I get bruised, so be it. I will ice them later. This feels- Fuck-" her words filter out as my pace quickens.

I grab another ice cube from the cup nearby and continue to rub it over her clit; the circles matching the pace of my thrusts. Her body convulses beneath me, and I feel the walls of her pussy tighten around my cock, making it hard to move at the same pace. She leans back and grinds into me, wanting me deeper, and when I feel the head of my dick hit her G-spot, I fucking lose it. With two more thrusts, my body convulses as I empty myself inside her.

Working On Us

"Nothing you confess
Could make me love you less"
–The Pretenders

Blake

"**I**'M NOT SURE WHAT I was thinking, Luke. Next time we get in a fight, can we start with this?" I chuckle as we lay in bed tangled in the sheets, our skin coated in sweat.

"You say that now because you're in a post sex bliss, B." Luke caresses my hair.

"No, I'm serious. Ana asked me what I was doing, and I couldn't answer her. I was more miserable with you gone than I was mad at you here." I sigh. "But for me, it was more than what you said, Luke. It was all the things you didn't say with words, but with your actions. You didn't need me."

"I need you. What do you mean?"

"When the accident happened, and you were at your lowest, you confided in everyone else, your parents, Isa, but held me at arm's length." A tear trickles down my cheek.

He drops his head. "B, all I needed was you, but I didn't know how to show it. I know how stressful opening the bar has been and then you compound that with your fight with April, it's a lot. It felt selfish to lean on you. I thought I was doing the right thing."

"I should have said something earlier." I sigh.

"You had every right to be pissed at me. I said things I didn't mean and I should have never said." He lays a gentle kiss on the top of my head. "But, B, you also need to fight fair."

"What?" I look up at him, genuinely curious about what he means by that. I place my hand on his to let him know we're good, I need to hear what he has to say. "You kind of backed me in a corner, B. One second you're upset that you thought I didn't need you, and then you're also upset that I wanted you to need me. I feel like I can't win sometimes."

I ponder what he says for a minute, and he's right.

I lay a gentle kiss on his lips and look up into his hazel eyes with every intention of demanding more of our kiss. My intentions are interrupted by his alarm. He groans.

"I thought you had today off," I protest as I pull the blankets over us and snuggle in.

"I do, but I have a therapy appointment in an hour. I won't be gone long. Stay right here. I'll bring breakfast home," he requests with subtle urgency.

"Luke, it's already 9:00. By the time you finish, it will be lunchtime." I roll into him. "I didn't know you were in therapy."

"I was in therapy after DJ died, and again while going through my divorce. I started going again after I spiraled when Adam came into the hospital. It resurfaced a lot of shit for me." His voice is low, laced with a tone I haven't heard before.

"I thought Adam was doing better?"

"He is, but with us still not talking, I kept going so I could work on myself. Be a better version of myself, this made me realize that I still have a lot to work through and that takes time. I have to allow myself the time." He sighs.

I get up and walk to the shower. "What are you doing?" he asks

"I think I'll go with you. We can work on ourselves, together as a couple. If nothing else, I'll wait outside and we can go get lunch afterwards," I suggest.

"I would love that. She urges her patients to bring family members with them to support the process. I'll talk to her when we get there." His smile brightens up the room.

We quickly get dressed, grab a coffee from the cart at the hospital, and now I'm sitting in the therapist's lobby's office waiting for Luke to come get me. The therapist said she wanted to meet with Luke alone, and then meet us together.

I take a slow sip of my coffee, the bitter warmth doing little to steady the frantic swirl of nerves bouncing around in my stomach like loose marbles. The idea of therapy has always felt distant. An abstract concept for other people. But now, sitting here, waiting, I feel the weight of what I'm about to step into. It's not just therapy. It's therapy with someone else, with Luke, a shared unraveling of truths I'm not sure we are ready to face. My hands tremble slightly when the therapist comes out and calls my name to join her and Luke in her office.

When I walk in the door, the first thing I notice is Luke standing facing me. The office is a blend of calm and clinical. I have no doubt it is designed to put you at ease without letting you forget you are here. Soft muted tones of beige and gray cover the walls, accented by two pieces of abstract artwork in gentle blues and greens. A pair of mid-century armchairs sits across from a plush oversized couch where Luke is standing. All of it angled around a small glass coffee table in the center. A faint scent of lavender drifts through the space, likely from a diffuser on a shelf nearby. There is a large window behind the chairs that lets in a great deal of natural light, even through the privacy of the tilted blinds.

I move next to Luke and we sit down next to each other, but he won't let go of my hand. "I'm Bella," the therapist says softly.

"Blake, nice to meet you," I introduce myself, my voice more steady than I expected it would be.

"Let's start with how you're feeling right now. Blake, you go first," Bella requests. She is an older woman, likely in her late fifties. She has dark hair with no traces of gray, but her eyes have light wrinkles in each corner. They are soft, as if formed overtime by smiling. Her words are very basic and straightforward, but her demeanor is soft and inviting. I see why Luke comes to see her.

"I'm a little nervous. I don't know what to expect." I turn to face Luke, "Have you done this before? I'm a little worried this could spark another fight between us." I gesture between us with a worried expression.

Luke shifts in his seat, clearly nervous about it too.

"What makes you think that?" Bella asks, writing something in her notepad.

"Well, part of working on a relationship is talking about things that have happened so you can move past them, and we're coming off a pretty big fight. We kind of broached the conversation earlier and it was good, we're good, but I'm still nervous."

"Was the fight big or were the feelings big?" she asks without taking her eyes off her notebook.

I pause. That's one way of looking at it that hadn't occurred to me. "I'm not sure."

"That's OK," she has a soft smile. "Tell me what happened that led to the big fight."

"There is a guy I met at a friend's wedding before Luke moved back here. We had a one-night stand, and I thought he was a pretty big jerk about it, and it made me question who I want to be, what I want for myself. Well, it turns out-" I look at Luke, not sure what I can divulge about Cash since he's volunteering here.

He reads my mind and interjects. "Cash," he confirms with a nod.

Ok, we divulge everything here.

"He knows Luke, and-well, long story short, we were not on good terms because of a misunderstanding. Luke was really upset when he heard my accounts of what I thought he said about me. When Cash showed up to the soft opening of my bar with April, Luke's sister, Luke lost it. They got into a fight and ruined the night. I was upset, but when we tried to talk about it the next morning emotions were high and Luke said some very hurtful things to me, so I packed a bag and left." I feel like I'm a little kid tattling right now.

"Where did you go?" she asks.

"The bar. I had to work."

"Were you going to stay there?"

"I don't actually know," I admit.

"What did he say that upset you?" Bella asks.

"All I needed from him was a free place to live." Luke shifts again in his seat, and I see him run his hands over his beard.

"Luke, what made you say that?" she asks.

He takes a long breath. "My ex wife was strong and independent, so much so that she never needed me. It's hard to explain, baby," he shifts towards me. "I love how independent you are, how much you can do for yourself. It's something I admire about you. But, when you tell me you don't need me to take care of you, or protect you, it guts me. I need you to need me. Otherwise, what will keep you with me?" He looks away.

I tighten my grip on his hand, hoping he will look at me. I decide it's better if I just say the quiet part out loud. "Luke, you-you will keep me with you. I love you. I'm not going to cheat on you or leave you. Baby, I don't *need* you to protect me and take care of me, but I *want* you to. I tried to tell you this before. Needing you means things like the soft opening will happen again, because you will feel the need to step in and take charge, protect me, because I can't do it myself, but I can. Luke, I am very sorry I lash out and have big reactions." I pause for a moment before continuing.

"But I finally understand how you feel, because I wanted you to need me too, but it just dawned on me, this is what we need to work on. We can't rely on each other to be complete, we're both perfect the way we are. Wanting you is a choice, needing you means I'm not enough on my own. Luke, I'm finally whole, and your presence, it just enhances my life. In so many ways. I chose you because you bring me joy, passion, and connection, and that's all I've always wanted." I shake my head, trying to register our conversation, empathizing with how broken he truly is. Luke carries things I didn't realize. Noel's cheating on him scarred his heart, even though he wasn't in love with her.

I get lost in this thought as Bella turns her attention to Luke. He is strong and confident and, most of the time, he is my voice of reason. But I realize he's more complicated than that. He is more broken than I realized and the thought peels back a small piece of armor I have built around my heart over the years, creating space for him I didn't realize he hadn't already occupied.

Five minutes ago I thought he held all of my heart, but at this moment I am realizing how much more I could love him.

But, shit, I'm scarred too. I never saw them until now

I understand why April was so worried about us coming together right now. She saw the scars and frayed edges that decorate both our hearts, ones only someone from the outside looking in with true love could see. I also realize how naïve I've been.

Love is not just being there for people how they want you, it's being there in the ways they need you, even if it's difficult and creates friction. This is a lot like the love most parents have for their children, a love I never experienced, so I couldn't recognize it in her and got pissed instead.

I don't know how to make things between us better, but I know listening to Luke and loving him is a step in the right direction.

I KNOW BEING INDEPENDENT is important to Blake. I know she was hesitant to move in with me, and felt like a freeloader. That made my words feel even more harsh.

"Why did you end up leaving the apartment, Luke?" Bella asks.

I turn to Blake, deciding to continue talking to her instead of Bella. "I knew you needed space, but over my dead body were you going to spend one night on someone's couch. You have been working so hard, and I am so proud of you. You deserved to be at home, comfortable in your own bed. I spend a lot of nights at the hospital, so it would have killed me knowing you were on some couch and the bed was empty."

She just smiles and grips my hand tighter. A slow burning wave of emotion builds within my chest, radiating through my body, and consumes me.

"B, fuck, I know this is not romantic and you deserve more than this moment, but you being here with me-it means more to me than you can imagine. I'm done mincing my words or waiting for the timing to be perfect. I fucking love you, B. I always have. When I look at you, the rest of the world fades away. The curve of your smile, the way your eyes crinkle around the edges when you laugh. I've etched every detail about you into my memory. I catalog everything you do and replay it repeatedly when we're apart. You are everything to me. Dammit-I'm sorry. I should have made sure we were alone when I said this out loud for the first time." I run my hands over my face, disappointed with my timing.

"Luke, stop," Blake says, pulling my hands away from my face. "I love you so fucking much. You're all I need. However you show up, that's what I need. Bella is onto something. I have so much shit built up with my mom and guys I've dated and I react big when the situation isn't that big to protect myself from being hurt. Our fight was not big enough that one of us had to leave. All I need is you, Luke, whatever it looks like for us, that's what I need."

I just stare at her for a second, not knowing how to proceed. I take in my surroundings. An apologetic smile is all I can offer Bella. "I'm going to kiss her, ok?"

Before Bella can respond, my hands wrap around Blake's jawline and I pull her into me. Our lips meet in a slow soft kiss, opening slightly like pieces of a puzzle. Placing my forehead against her, I pull away just enough to see her glossy eyes. "B, I love you so much. I'm really sorry I ruined your opening day. I promise I will spend the rest of my life making it up to you."

"I can't wait to see what that's like." She bites her lower lip, a smile tugging at her mouth.

Her eyes soften, and for the first time in what feels like forever, the tension between us begins to ease.I don't know what I expected her to say, but when she reaches for my hand, it's enough. The apology, the forgive-ness-everything feels like it's finally starting to fall into place.

What If We Can Have It All?

Three months later...

"All we need is just the two of us"
-Shania Twain

Blake

L&L is fully running, and Amari is literally a lifesaver. I couldn't do this without her. I get pulled in so many directions, I'm not at the bar as often as I'd like. She spent the entire day stocking the shelves and inventorying every single book, every bottle, and ordered new bar glasses to replace ones accidentally broken by customers. I know it would be cheaper if I ordered plastic ones; yes, they look like glass, but it feels cheap to me. I enjoy the feel of heavy glass in my hand when enjoying a glass of wine or a cocktail.

I got here about an hour ago and sent her with my card to grab us some dinner. There are a few customers relaxing in various reading nooks, and as the sun sets, many of their latte orders have shifted to libations of sorts. Since Christmas time is my favorite, there is a large tree in the center of the room. Its warm lights cast a comforting glow and the gold and red ornaments decorating the branches make it have a cozy feel. All the drinks being served are holiday themed, and a customer favorite, the

Eggnog Martini, is Luke's creation. It's a vodka eggnog with amaretto and nutmeg, garnished with a cinnamon stick. I've made more of them in the last week than I can count.

I walk over to the shelves to put away a few stray books that were left on tables or in seating areas over the course of the week. I also have a few books for the lost and found, and after one month, we place them in a basket on the bar accompanied by a sign that reads "The Lost Library-these books have lost their home. Can you help them find one?" hoping they can find a new home. It doesn't happen very often, but occasionally there will be a book left behind, seeking a new owner.

After I retrieved more limes for the girls tending the bar, I got distracted unpacking the boxes in the back. My thoughts drifted to the last time I celebrated Christmas with Luke. Only that time he belonged to someone else. A light clicking noise snaps me back to the present.

I look at the clock, noting Amari has been gone for about 45 minutes. The ramen place we often order from is just around the corner, so I'm a little worried it's taking her so long. I grab my phone and dial her number as I walk out into the main area, my heart rate picking up when I walk out to find the bar eerily empty. I wasn't in the back very long!

When I went to the back, there were still several cus-tomers in the store. I swear both the girls were definitely mixing drinks-now everyone, including my employ-ees, is gone.

What in the hell is going on?

Nervous, I dial Amari again, but it rings once and I'm sent to voicemail. Being in the bar alone has never worried me. This is a pretty safe area, but an eerie, unsettling feeling is invading my body, and my skin feels like it is crawling. I pick up my pace as I cross the room to lock the front door, and just as I reach for the lock, a familiar song replaces the instrumental Christmas music playing. I no longer hear "Santa Claus is Coming to Town" but a song by Shania Twain, "From This Moment On." When I turn around, Luke is leaning against the bar.

How did he get there?

I watch him as I move closer, not knowing what to say. He is in a navy suit, obviously tailored for every muscle in his arms. It's a suit with a white shirt, the top two buttons undone. He is wearing tan shoes to match the belt around his waist exactly.

Luke has style, but he never matches this well.

As I get closer, the smell of cedar and mint swirl around me, making me weak in the knees. I have so many thoughts floating around in my head, but the look on his face tells me this isn't the time to ask questions.

"Hi baby," I greet him by placing a soft kiss on his cheek.

He instantly wraps his arm around me, pulling me close to his body. "Hey, B."

He leans down and places a soft kiss on my lips and hands me the glass next to his arm propped on the bar. I lazily bring it to my lips and when the apple whisky and ginger ale slide over my tongue, a warm sensation follows behind the liquid, spreading through my body. I close my eyes and take in the feeling. When I open my eyes and move to set my drink down, there is a red velvet box with the most beautiful ring I have ever seen delicately placed inside.

Taking in the ring, time stands still. A band crafted from shimmering rose gold, sleek and bold, its warm pink hue radiating a soft romantic glow. In its center sits a striking black diamond. The smooth surface is polished, absorbing the soft light rather than reflecting it. The inky depths of the diamond create a dramatic contrast to the rose gold band, giving it an air of sophistication.

It's simple.

Modern.

Yet, timeless.

I find it hard to tear my eyes away from the beautifully crafted masterpiece and focus on the other masterpiece in front of me. Luke's whisky eyes are glassy and have a sense of longing in them radiating from their vast depths. His eyes communicate everything.

He takes the ring from the velvet chest and silently brings it to my hand and slides in onto my ring finger. It's a perfect fit. Of course it is. Luke's attention to detail is unmatched, and one thing he would hate more than anything else is giving me a ring I couldn't wear, one I'd have to wait to have fitted. I'm not sure how he knew my ring size, but right now, it's not important.

We are standing in an intimate charged silence.

He still has not said a word, but the love he pours into me sends a tremor of raw emotion directly to the depths of my soul.

A single tear slides down my cheek.

$$\mathcal{Luke}$$

I SILENTLY WIPE THE tear from Blake's cheek with the knuckle of my index finger, gently unfolding it as the pad runs over her perfect red lips. As it passes, she lays a feather-like kiss against my skin, making goosebumps move over my body like waves crashing on the shore.

She is absolute perfection, her red hair in loose curls toppling over her shoulders, her eyes sparkling in the light on the nearby Christmas tree, the scent of vanilla and honey circling around me.

I had a plan, a speech ready, but the moment I saw her, everything disappeared. All of my words vanished like smoke coming off a cigar-fleeting.

I place another kiss on her lips, claiming them with just a touch. When I pull away, her eyes are shimmering like glass marbles, coated in tears that have yet to leave the comfort of her brilliant eyes.

I swallow the lump building in my throat. "Be my wife, B."

It's not a question. Questions are for things you don't know the answer to. This is a request for the inevitable.

"Yes." She smiles and then her lips are on mine again.

At this moment, everything is right. Everything is exactly how it's meant to.

I can't wait to change her name-to hear it come off her lips when she introduces herself; Blake Jennings-two words always meant to sit side by side. She's finally going to be my wife, and there is nothing that can stop me from worshiping her, this time around.

Acknowledgements

ALRIGHT, BUCKLE UP, BECAUSE I have a lot of 'thank you's' to dish out!

First off, to all the readers who picked up this book (or downloaded it, or maybe just saw it on a shelf and thought, "Huh, that cover looks fun"), I owe you a massive thank you! You guys are the real MVPs. Without your support, I'd just be talking to myself, which, okay, I do a lot, but it's way more fun when you're involved.

To my incredible team at Good Girls PR, Lindsey and Shaye, you are the wizardry behind the curtain, the magic that makes everything look effortless. Thank you for turning my messy ideas into something actually readable and making sure people know it exists. You're like the behind-the-scenes superheroes I never knew I needed (but now can't live without).

To my beta readers, Bella, Aimee, Brooke, and Alyssa, where do I even start? You didn't just read the book; you dissected it like you were on a mission. Your feedback was everything. I don't know if you realize this, but you're basically my writing life coaches. You kept me from making a total mess of things (mostly). You're the real reason this book isn't just a bunch of random thoughts and coffee stains.

And to my husband, who somehow puts up with my "I'm busy writing" face (which is just me staring at the screen like a zombie) and listens to me rant about characters like they're real people. Thank you for being my emotional support human, my snack provider, and the person who gently reminded me to go outside and remember what sunlight looks like.

To everyone who's been a part of this crazy ride, thank you, thank you, thank you! You're the best. Now, go grab a drink and celebrate because we did this together!

www.ingramcontent.com/pod-product-compliance
Lightning Source LLC
Chambersburg PA
CBHW020234010826
48973CB00006B/1505